PISTOL LAW

Center Point
Large Print

Books are
produced in the
United States
using U.S.-based
materials

Books are printed
using a revolutionary
new process called
THINKtech™ that
lowers energy usage
by 70% and increases
overall quality

Books are
durable and
flexible
because of
Smyth-sewing

Paper is
sourced using
environmentally
responsible
foresting methods
and the
paper is acid-free

Also by Paul Evan Lehman and available from
Center Point Large Print:

Cowhand Justice

**This Large Print Book carries the
Seal of Approval of N.A.V.H.**

PISTOL LAW

Paul Evan Lehman

CENTER POINT LARGE PRINT
THORNDIKE, MAINE

This Center Point Large Print edition
is published in the year 2019 by arrangement with
Golden West Literary Agency.

Originally published in the US by
Quinn Publishing Company, Inc.
Originally published in the UK by Linford.

The text of this Large Print edition is unabridged.
In other aspects, this book may vary
from the original edition.
Printed in the United States of America
on permanent paper.
Set in 16-point Times New Roman type.

ISBN: 978-1-64358-168-2 (hardcover)
ISBN: 978-1-64358-172-9 (softcover)

Library of Congress Cataloging-in-Publication Data

Names: Lehman, Paul Evan, author.
Title: Pistol law / Paul Evan Lehman.
Description: Center Point Large Print edition. | Thorndike, Maine :
    Center Point Large Print, 2019.
Identifiers: LCCN 2019002326| ISBN 9781643581682 (hardcover :
    alk. paper) | ISBN 9781643581729 (paperback : alk. paper)
Subjects: LCSH: Large type books. | GSAFD: Western stories.
Classification: LCC PS3523.E434 P48 2019 | DDC 813/.54—dc23
LC record available at https://lccn.loc.gov/2019002326

One

He was thinking as he rode along the street that Mustang had certainly changed. He had been in the town just once before this and that was four years ago, but he had every reason to remember it and his memory was of a drab and dirty little cowtown different from others of its size only in the arrogance and brutality of those of its inhabitants it had been his misfortune to meet.

He noticed first of all the plank sidewalks. There had been no sidewalks at all four years ago. He saw too that most of the buildings had been recently painted and that several new and pretentious homes had been built. That brick building on the corner opposite the hotel was new also. His eyes went to the sign over its door and he reined his horse to a sudden stop.

The First Bank of Rossiter. Rossiter! Had he made a mistake in the town? Four years ago its name had been Mustang. He glanced quickly about him, then let his gaze go to the broad valley beyond the village. No, he had made no mistake; but why Rossiter?

He rode to the hotel and tied his horse at the rack and went into the lobby. This had once been the Mustang Hotel and now it was the Taylor House, but it was the same one he had entered so hopefully on that momentous evening. A young man with a wisp of moustache and an imitation carnation in his buttonhole was behind the desk and he remembered him too, and recognition brought a tingling sensation at the back of his neck as the hackles rose.

The clerk looked down a long nose, noticed the dusty Stetson, plain dark coat and bullhide chaps and decided that this was a cowboy riding the grub line. He inquired coolly, "Yes?"

"Supper and quarters for myself and my horse."

The clerk nodded towards a registry book, said, "Sign there," and turned to the key rack. The young man's name was Lancelot Jefferson Jones; he wrote L. J. Jones, hesitated a moment, then added Tombstone, Ariz. The clerk put a key on the counter, swung the book about and glanced at the signature. He gave a slight start and raised his eyes to observe L. J. Jones more closely.

He saw a tall, well setup young man of twenty-three, wide of shoulder and narrow of waist, with tanned and smooth-shaven cheeks, curly brown hair and blue eyes fringed with heavy lashes. At the moment the face was set in harsh lines and the eyes were frosty. L. J. Jones said, "I want the best room in the house."

The clerk said, "Yes, sir," and reached for

another key. "Number one; right in the front. That'll be two dollars."

Lance Jones said, "I'll settle up when I leave," and went outside. He led his horse around to the stable, turned him over to a hostler with instructions for his care, unstrapped his bedroll and carried it up to his room. He felt the eyes of the clerk follow him up the stairs and he smiled faintly and the frosty look went out of his eyes. The Tombstone had done it; Tombstone was a tough town and it was the part of wisdom to treat its citizens with respect.

He had just finished brushing his clothes and washing up when the supper bell rang. He went down to the dining room and found a seat at the long table. There were half a dozen others present and he examined them as he ate. Among them were two men he remembered having seen in the lobby on that other night; one was a heavy-set man with sideburns and moustache and the other his counterpart but some twenty-five years younger. Both bore a resemblance to the supercilious clerk at the hotel desk, and Lance decided that the older man was the owner of the hotel and the younger ones his sons. The two at the table were watching him furtively but he was quite sure they had not recognized him. Considering the appearance he had made on that other evening it would have been a miracle if they had.

A man came into the dining room and stood just inside the doorway looking about him. He was a big, heavy man with a red face and ragged moustache and he stood with his thumbs hooked in the armholes of his vest so that the pushed-back coat revealed the marshal's shield on his chest.

Lance felt the blood throb in his temples and his grip tightened on the table knife he was holding. Well he remembered this man. He even knew his name. It was Dave Schultz and it was he who had once held a gun at Lance's back as he walked along the street to the edge of town. Lance lowered his eyes and worked on a piece of steak until he had control of his emotions. When he looked up again Dave Schultz's hard gaze was on him. Lance returned it with one just as hard and presently Dave let his glance go elsewhere. He came over to the table and sat down.

One by one the other diners finished and left, but Lance ate leisurely, hoping that others he had seen that night would come in. None did. Schultz, wolfing his food, finished as Lance rose from the table and was close to him as he went into the lobby. The marshal asked, "Stranger in town, ain't you?"

"You should know; you're the marshal."

Schultz scowled. "Don't be funny. We don't like funny fellers in Rossiter."

"I don't like nosey marshals."

They faced each other, exchanging cold stares. Schultz growled, "Keep your nose clean while you're in town." He nodded shortly and slouched through the doorway and across the veranda.

Lance turned to the clerk. "Seems to me that I heard this town called Mustang. Anything wrong with my ears?"

The clerk shook his head. "The name used to be Mustang. It was changed three years or so ago. It was named after Mr. Mark Rossiter, our mayor and president of the bank."

Lance nodded his comprehension and went outside. A horseman had just dismounted before the hotel and was coming up the steps, a medium sized man, but broad shouldered and strong, a few years older than Lance. He had bold black eyes, a waxed moustache, and there was an arrogant tilt to his head. He was wearing a rather ornate cowman's outfit and his rig sported plenty of horse jewelry. Lance stiffened and once more the hackles rose. He remembered this man, too.

The fellow gave him a casual glance and passed into the lobby. Lance heard him greet the clerk behind the desk. "Hello, Ed. Going to the shindig tonight?"

"Good evening, Ben. Yes, I hope to. George and I will be over when the governor relieves me. Somewhere between eight and eight-thirty."

Lance sat down in a chair and rolled a cigarette. He watched the passersby as he smoked, hoping to see still others of the crowd that had been in the hotel that night four years before. He saw nobody whom he recognized. The dusk gathered and presently the young man called Ben came out. Now he was dressed as he had been on that other evening, in clothes of Eastern fashion and cut. He went jauntily down the steps and walked up the street. Lance, curious to see where he went in that rig, followed him.

Ben reached the Wildcat Saloon, glanced over the doors as he was about to pass, then turned and went inside. When Lance entered Ben had just reached the bar. Marshal Dave Schultz was there and had turned to greet him and Ben pushed into place beside him, roughly shouldering a little, wizened old man out of his way. Lance heard the old fellow say sharply, "Watch where you're goin', Ben Clark."

Ben turned his head, saw who had spoken, gave the old fellow a contemptuous glance and ordered whiskey. Lance took a place beside the old man and bought a drink for himself. The old fellow mumbled, "Danged stuck-up pup!"

Ben Clark, his attention on the marshal at his left, snatched up the drink the bartender had poured, and as he raised it his elbow struck the old man's shoulder and some of the whiskey splashed over the rim of the glass and onto his

10

coat. He cried, "Damn you, Abner!" and with a quick flick of his wrist threw the remaining whiskey into the old fellow's face.

Abner staggered against Lance, who steadied him and spoke sharply over his shoulder. "The man wasn't to blame; you did it yourself."

Abner shook himself free, dabbed at his face with a coat sleeve, then threw a wild right which Ben deflected with his arm. Lance saw Ben's face harden and cold rage come into his eyes. Ben muttered. "You asked for it, you old coot!" and came around with a left which caught Abner on the side of the jaw and sent him sprawling.

"And you asked for this!" said Lance, and came up with an uppercut which caught Ben squarely on the point of the chin.

Ben was knocked backwards against the marshal, who threw his arms about him to keep his balance. Ben slipped through them and to the floor. He lay there, completely out. Schultz cried, "Dang you, feller! I told you—!" He made a stab for the gun at his hip.

He never got it clear of the holster. A hard fist caught him flush on the mouth and he staggered backwards, grabbing at the bar. Lance was after him like a cat, seizing his gun hand and tearing it away from the weapon. He twisted swiftly and Schultz spun about to escape the torture, and when he had turned, Lance thrust the bent arm upward, holding the marshal powerless. He said tightly, "You're not in on this play, Schultz. There are too many witnesses for you to arrest me on a frameup."

Somebody at the far end of the bar called, "That's right, pilgrim! We all seen what happened." There was a chorus of affirmation. It was evident that the marshal of Rossiter was not a popular man.

"You heard them," said Lance. "This ends right here; understand?"

Schultz made a futile heave, failed to break Lance's hold and growled, "I savvy. You get away with it this time."

Lance let go his arm and stepped back a pace. Abner had picked himself up and was glaring. Schultz turned slowly, his ruddy face redder than normal, his eyes glinting with rage. Lance watched him warily, poised, ready to rush him if he made another move towards his gun. Schultz glared for a moment, then spat and delivered himself.

"No man makes a monkey of me and gets away with it. I warned you to keep your nose clean while you're in this man's town, and I'll be watchin' you. Step out of line just one little inch and I'll put you where you'll cool off mighty sudden. Either in jail or on an undertaker's slab."

"I don't like jails," Lance told him shortly. "As for the slab, I'll be wearing a gun the next time we meet. Meanwhile, I'll keep an eye on all the dark alleys."

"I'm no bushwhacker," declared Schultz angrily. "And when I shoot, the other feller always gets his chance. You step out of line and you'll get yours." They traded glares for another few seconds, then Schultz shook his head for emphasis and turned away. He slouched along the bar and went out into the darkness.

Ben Clark had regained consciousness and was sitting up holding his jaw. He sat there for a short space, then got slowly to his feet, leaned against the bar and said thickly, "Give me a drink."

He downed the whiskey, set the glass on the bar and turned his head to look at Lance. He said, "I'll remember this, pilgrim."

"I hope you do," Lance said grimly.

Ben leaned over unsteadily and picked up the derby hat he had dropped. He brushed the sawdust from it, set it on his head and strode towards the entrance. He wobbled a bit as he walked.

Abner muttered, "A derby! Wish I'd put my foot through it." His glance went to Jones. "Friend, this calls for a drink. Belly up."

They had the drink. Lance asked, "Who's the fellow who knocked you down?"

"Name of Ben Clark. Him and his old man run a two-bit ranch in the valley." He flashed

13

Lance an apprehensive glance. "I'm obliged to you for what you done, friend, but you hadn't oughta horned in. Ben stands in with the powers that be and you've done made trouble for yourself."

"That will suit me just fine. I came here hunting trouble. My name's Jones; Lance Jones."

"Proud to meet up with you, Jones. I'm Abner Stacy." They shook hands gravely.

"I understand they've changed the name of the town to Rossiter."

Abner spat. "Yeah; but it'll always be Mustang to me."

"I'd like to know about it. And some other things. Maybe you can tell me."

"Feller, I shore can. Been livin' here off'n on for twenty years. I sure can tell you plenty of hist'ry."

"Who's this man Mark Rossiter and where does he live?"

"He come from the East four years ago, started up a bank, built him a smackin' big house and sent back East for his wife and daughter. When they come out they fetched a passel of dam' Yanks with 'em. He lives—I can show you a heap easier'n I can tell you. Feel like walkin' up the street a piece?"

"Sure. Let's go."

"Dave Schultz and Ben went out the front way, mebbe we'd better sorta slip out by the rear."

"We'll go right out the front. They won't start anything now; they were in the wrong and there were too many witnesses."

They walked up the street together and presently Abner said, "There it is; that big house standin' back from the street. And there's somethin' goin' on; party, I reckon. They're always havin' 'em."

They halted near the front gate. The house was lighted up and the front door stood open. Just within the vestibule stood a big, important appearing man with a glinting brown beard, a short, stout woman who carried a lorgnette, and a slim girl with pale hair and a poker face.

"The aristocracy of Mustang," said Abner. "Mark Rossiter and his wife and daughter. Mark's our dishonorable mayor and president of our local lootin' establishment. The she male hipperpotamus is his wife and the thin drink of water their offspring, Stella. Some pumpkins, ain't they?"

"I take it you're not one of Rossiter's upper crust, oldtimer."

"You take it plumb correct. They's twelve of 'em that run this yere town, countin' two old maid sisters that sorta drifted in with the tide. Me and the rest of the townsfolk have got to hate 'em. They've corralled the business and the money of this yere town and they ain't a thing we can do."

"That bad, eh?" said Lance softly. The opinion he had formed of this crowd was being confirmed.

"Yes, sir. And worse. Was a time when you could live in Mustang free like God intended you to; now you pay taxes. Taxes for the mayor and his handpicked council, taxes for sidewalks, taxes for a marshal. Hell! What's a town this size doin' with a mayor and town council? And if they're needed why don't they serve without pay? And why don't the merchants and saloonkeepers chip in and pay a marshal if the town's so danged wicked it needs one?"

"And it was they who changed the name from Mustang to Rossiter?"

"Yeah. Oh, they put it up to the voters, but we weren't wise to 'em then and folks didn't care whether their mail come to Mustang or Rossiter or Patagonia because they never got none to amount to anything. But they're a bunch of greedy, graspin' dam' Yankees, and they hang together. Take turns throwin' fancy parties like this one yere, and respectable Western clothes ain't good enough for 'em. I betcha if you slapped a Stetson on Mark Rossiter's head he'd die of mortification. Why, they even have afternoon teas! *Teas!* Good gosh and the cows come home!"

Lance slipped an arm over the old fellow's shoulders. "Abner, I believe you and I are going

16

to put a crimp in their tails. Who are those people going in now?"

"The two shakin' hands with Rossiter and his overstuffed spouse are Jacob Ordman and his wife. Ordman's a lawyer and got hisself made manager of Nancy Pendleton's Stars and Bars ranch out in the valley. The two fellers followin' 'em in are Henry and Jack, their sons, and the gal is Sue Ordman, their daughter."

"Nancy Pendleton," mused Lance. His face had tightened. "I want to know all about her, too. Abner, where can we do some talking?"

"Down at my shack. Got a quart of Kentuck bourbon and we'll see what we can do about killin' it."

"That suits me fine. I've got a bad taste in my mouth."

"You'n me both. Come along."

Abner's shack turned out to be a very neat little cabin, strictly the home of a widower. He told Lance on the way there that he had made a pretty good strike some ten years before and was taking it easy now, going on occasional prospecting trips merely to keep his hand in. His wife had been dead for a great many years and he had one son, the foreman of a cow outfit in Texas. Abner had wanted to set the young man up in business but Joe Stacy was determined to earn his own stake.

Abner got out the quart of Kentucky bourbon and they drank to each other's health; then Abner said, "What do you want me to tell you, Lance?"

"Everything. First the Pendletons, then these hombres who have taken over the town."

"Wal, the Pendletons come here from Kentucky right after the war between the states. They're real quality and the old man was a colonel in Gen'ral Lee's army. He lost everything in the war, but his son Nathan married a rich gal and they bought a big chunk of land in the valley and started the Stars and Bars cow ranch."

"They bought it? It's not free range?"

"Bought it from *Señor* Don Esteban Guiterras, who owned the whole valley under a Spanish grant. Don Esteban's a Spanish gentleman and there was a time when he was right prosperous; but his sons got married and drifted down into Mexico and now the old gent's all alone."

"Think he'd consider selling more of his land?"

Abner flashed him a quick glance. "You know somebody that'd be interested in buyin'?"

"Yes. One my reasons for coming here was to find land in the valley for a cattle company."

"Wal, I reckon you might make a deal with Don Esteban. His place is runnin' down and you know how them old fellers are—figger the Lord will provide for them as their due. Yes, sir, you might swing it."

"Go on about the Pendletons."

18

"Wal, there's the Colonel, and there's his granddaughter Nancy. Nancy was born on the Stars and Bars and her ma died when she was a kid. Her father was killed four, five years ago when his hoss fell into a ravine with him. Wasn't much of a fall, but somehow he managed to land underneath his hoss and had his chest crushed.

"He'd built up the Stars and Bars into a big spread and he left it to Nancy with the Colonel to manage it until she got married or was twenty-one. The Colonel is a gent of the old school somethin' like Don Esteban. Thinks that money grows on trees that bloom the year round, proud and dignified and got no head a-tall for such vulgar things as business and finance. He's been runnin' the spread since Nate got killed, and when I say runnin' I mean runnin' it into the ground."

"Poor manager?"

"No manager a-tall. Used to plantation ways and leavin' everything to his crew and to Jake Ordman, who talked hisself into managin' the finances of the ranch. Nancy's the apple of his eye and they ain't nothin' too good for her. Fust thing he done was ship her off to a high-toned school for young ladies in Louisville. Takes money to keep a gal away from home and at a fancy school like that. Ain't only her board and lodgin' and the cost of her schoolin', which is high enough, but she's got to do a lot of entertainin' and buy a lot of clothes and keep a ridin' hoss and gosh knows what all."

"And the ranch pays for it."

"The ranch *will* pay for it in the long run. When she's home on her vacations it's jest one round of merriment. Parties every other night at the ranch, or the Rossiters, or the Ordmans, or one of the others; trips to the cities for shoppin' and shows and suchlike. Money sure flies."

"Must be a prosperous ranch."

"Must be. Of course, when the Colonel needs cash he don't sell off a bunch of steers; he goes to Jake Ordman and signs a note and Jake runs down to the bank and gets the cash. Don't know what he does when the notes come due, but he must pay off or a shark like Rossiter wouldn't lend him no more."

"What are the Pendletons like?"

"You mean looks? Wal, the Colonel is tall and slim and active for a feller of his age. Must be crowdin' seventy. Always dresses elegant and is dignified as all getout. White hair and bushy white brows and sharp black eyes. Wears a moustache and goatee like Gen'ral Custer. Nancy—wal, she's just plain beautiful. About twenty, I reckon. Nice brown hair and eyes that are sorta violet. But bad spoiled. All I got ag'in either of 'em is their mixin' with this crowd of tinhorns in town. They'll get contaminated in time."

"I suppose. Nancy's still in school?"

"Graddiates next month. Colonel's gone there to be with her and see her commence. He'll fetch her back."

"Now tell me about the Yankee invasion."

"Invasion is right! Mark Rossiter come to Mustang about four years ago, hung around awhile and then said he aimed to settle down and make a real mee-tropolis outa Mustang. He opened a bank and built a big house and when it was finished he sent for his wife and daughter. And when they come out they brought a whole passel of friends with 'em.

"Jake Ordman opened a law office, feller named Caleb Bennett started a hardware store, Percy Dunn opened a barber shop and Leander Taylor bought the Mustang Hotel and renamed it the Taylor House. Two old gals named Luella and Pricilla Hargrave started up a dressmakin' and millinery establishment. They're more or less harmless."

"Describe them to me, Abner."

Abner flashed him another look; he knew these questions were not being asked merely to make conversation. He went on to describe each in turn. He had already pointed out Rossiter, his wife and daughter, and Ordman and his family. Leander Taylor had two sons, Edward and George, whom Lance had already identified. Caleb Bennett had a wife, a daughter Clara and a son named Tom. Percy Dunn was a widower with two daughters, Gloria and Elsie.

They had another drink when Abner had finished and for a short space there was silence; then Lance said, "There's one you left out. Where does Ben Clark fit into the picture?"

"Oh, him! Like I told you, him and his father run a two-bit ranch on the edge of the Stars and Bars. Bought a quarter-section from Don Esteban and graze their cows on the Don's range. Got his eye on Nancy Pendleton and hangs around with the town bunch. Prob'ly keeps his old man broke buyin' clothes and entertainin'. They come from Illinois."

Lance said, "I wanted to know all about them for a particular reason. I saw the whole bunch once before and formed my opinion of them. I wanted to be sure I hadn't made a mistake."

Abner was staring at him. He said slowly, "You're a Westerner, Lance, and you dress like a cowhand; but danged if you don't talk like a perfessor. Rossiter and his bunch can sure spout words, but you could give 'em cards and spades and big casino and still trim 'em."

"I've been studying in the East for the past three and half years, Abner; but I'm a Westerner, all right. Born in Tennessee and came out here with my folks when I was just a little shaver. I'm sure obliged for what you've told me. Some time I may tell you why I hate Rossiter and his bunch and why I'm determined to hurt them as much as I can."

"I ain't askin' no questions," said Abner, "but if you aim to do some tail twistin' I'd sure like to horn in on the deal."

"You will, Abner. I'll let you know when it's time. Now I'll amble down to the hotel. I'll see you later. Good night."

At the Rossiter home the younger folks were having a taffy pulling party in the kitchen; the elder women had gathered in the parlour for a bit of polite gossip, and the men were in Rossiter's study ostensibly for the purpose of sipping brandy and smoking. Had anyone gone to summon them he would have found the door securely locked.

Mark Rossiter, exuding prosperity and dignity, sat behind his desk; before him in chairs sat Jacob Ordman, Caleb Bennett, Leander Taylor and Percy Dunn. Rossiter had just called the meeting to order; now he looked at the faces before him much as an austere schoolmaster would regard his pupils before making some portentous announcement.

He spoke slowly, heavily. "A little over three years ago we organized the Rossiter Development Company. I had realized at once that the land at this end of the valley, properly irrigated, would make excellent farms which could be sold to Northern farmers at an immense profit. I sent for you in order that you might participate in the venture.

"At that time I had assumed that the land could be purchased from the Pendletons for an insignificant amount; after you arrived I was surprised to learn that the Colonel would not sell, having some foolish notion that he should turn over the property intact to his grand-daughter. In spite of this setback we organized and determined to mark time pending the securing of the land by other methods. Legal ones, of course. It has taken longer than we had anticipated, but the waiting was well worth while. I am happy to report that the steps taken will soon bear fruit. In a matter of a few months a strip of land a mile wide and extending across the valley for six miles will be ours. It will be subdivided into farms, the creek will be diverted so that its water can be carried by ditches to any part of the land, and we will be ready to go ahead with our sales."

The men seated before him exchanged pleased glances. Leander Taylor said, "You've done a nice job, Mark. We know that the Colonel has been encouraged to borrow money and that you have wisely let the debts accumulate instead of demanding payment when the notes were due, and I can see that the amount you've lent him must be a bit staggering; but the Pendletons graze a lot of cattle. What is to prevent the Colonel selling off enough stock to pay those notes when you call the loans?"

Rossiter smiled blandly and turned to Jacob Ordman. "I believe Jacob can explain that, Leander."

Ordman said shortly. "It's simple. The Colonel simply doesn't own as many cattle as he thinks he does. His herds have shrunk to about half of what his last roundup tally shows."

They looked shocked. Caleb Bennett exclaimed. "Do you mean to tell me that we've been *stealing* his cattle?"

"A better word would be *confiscating*," said Rossiter smiling. "Explain to them, Jacob."

"The thing to remember," said Ordman in that same hard voice, "is that both Pendleton and his son were officers in the Confederate Army. They were and are traitors to their country. They deserve no consideration whatever from loyal citizens like ourselves. If the Pendletons are ruined by our project I would rejoice in it as a victory for the Union."

The shocked looks left their faces; they were patriots, not thieves.

"That's logical," said Taylor. "It's time we showed these rebels we can outwit them just as easily as we outfought them."

"How did you manage it?" asked Percy Dunn.

"Why hasn't the Colonel noticed the shrinkage in his herds?"

"The Colonel hasn't noticed his losses because he leaves everything connected with the running of the ranch to his crew. One of my first steps as his financial adviser was to suggest the hiring of a new crew under Buck Borden. That crew, under the direction of Ben Clark, has been systematically looting the Stars and Bars for over three years. The details don't matter; it's sufficient to say that the Company is not involved at all. If anything should go wrong the whole blame can be pinned on Clark and Borden."

"Then you say we shall be ready to come out into the open within the next few months?" asked Caleb Bennett.

"Perhaps sooner than that," assured Rossiter. "We have been forced to keep the existence of our Company a secret even from our families for fear that the Colonel might learn of our desire to get that land. That secrecy must be maintained. I can't be too emphatic about that. If the Pendletons have an inkling of what is to happen they will base the price of the land on its equivalent in fertile, well watered farm land instead of barren range. Is that clearly understood?"

It was. They assured him of their continued silence.

He went on. "Then that about concludes the matter. For the past six months we have been advertising in Eastern papers suggesting that farmers who wanted to get in on the ground floor get in touch with the Rossiter Development Company. Our postmaster, Leander Taylor, has seen to it that the answers to those advertisements have come directly to me without falling under the eye of another person. We must move carefully until we secure title to the land.

"Everything is quite legal. At the proper time payment will be demanded and the Colonel will learn of the shrinkage of his herds. We will accuse him of making a false statement as to their number when he gave us a chattel mortgage on them, and will finally compromise by accepting that strip of land in lieu of so many cows. Then we can go to work in earnest."

A timid knock sounded on the door and the voice of Mrs. Rossiter reached them. "Mark, dear, refreshments are about to be served."

The meeting of the Rossiter Development Company stood adjourned.

Lance checked out of the Taylor House the next morning and rode westward into the valley where he found a trail which he judged to lead to the hacienda of Don Esteban Guiterras. Some five miles away, at the base of the northern hills, was a cluster of buildings which marked the site of the Stars and Bars ranch; a short distance beyond the Pendleton house was a smaller group of buildings which he judged belonged to the Clarks.

It was midmorning when he rode into the yard of Don Esteban's *hacienda* and Guiterras himself was seated in a big chair on the gallery. As Lance approached the old Spaniard rose with graceful dignity and clapped his hands and a servant came from the house to take Lance's horse. Lance mounted the steps, removed his hat respectfully and said, "My name is Lance Jones; I have the honor of addressing the *Señor* Don Esteban Guiterras?"

"That is correct, *Señor* Jones. My poor *casa* is yours."

A servant fetched them drinks and they sat facing each other conversing on subjects dealing with the weather, cattle and the world in general. When these preliminaries had been gone through with, Don Esteban asked politely, "The *Señor* Jones wishes to discuss some business with me, no?"

The *Señor* Jones immediately got down to brass tacks. He told Don Esteban that he knew of a cattle company which was desirous of purchasing land in the valley. He was fully aware that this was the ancestral home of Don Esteban, who undoubtedly was greatly attached to it; at the same time he also understood that Don

Esteban was now alone while his children lived in Mexico. Perhaps Don Esteban felt a natural longing to be with those he loved and a growing desire to be free of the endless details connected with the management of such a huge estate. In that case he might be willing to dispose of some or all of his land.

He noticed the momentary flash of the black eyes, but otherwise the old Spaniard gave no sign of elation. He nodded gravely and admitted that at times he was indeed tempted to consider an offer. He was an old man and, as the *Señor* Jones had observed, he often yearned for the companionship of his children and their *niños*. But he would require time to consider and undoubtedly the *Señor* Jones would wish to survey the property before making an offer.

The upshot of the whole matter was that Lance was persuaded to remain overnight as Don Esteban's guest while the old man considered. They spent the afternoon and most of the next day riding about on a tour of inspection, the Don sitting his beautifully rigged horse with the erectness of the born rider.

During the course of their inspection Lance said, "I notice many cattle wearing the brands of the Stars and Bars and the Circle C. You have perhaps some arrangement with their owners whereby they may use your range?"

"Not what you call the arrangement, *Señor*.

The range is here, too much for my own needs; they are welcome to its use."

"They do not pay you rental? You are generous, Don Esteban."

Don Esteban shrugged. "There was a time when the Guiterras herds needed the whole of the valley, but when my sons left me the burden became too great. I sold land to the Pendletons and the Clarks, I cut down the size of my herds. And now I think I am wearied of it. I have decided. I will sell your company everything and will rejoin my children."

So it came about that when at last Lance made his formal adieus a bargain had been struck and a substantial sum paid to bind it. Two days later Don Esteban would journey to Junction City where Lance would meet him to conclude the purchase and receive the deed. That deed would be executed in favor of the Avenger Cattle Company. Lance was very proud of that name.

Lance rode slowly, following the trail which paralleled the creek, and at noon he camped among the trees, staked out his horse on some grass, and ate the provisions which Don Esteban had insisted he take with him. When he had finished he moved to the edge of the trees, found a seat on a stone and smoked, enjoying the serenity and quiet.

The road to Rossiter was under his observation

and presently he saw a buckboard emerge from town and come bouncing along it. There were two men in the vehicle and the driver turned off the road about a mile from the town and headed northward over the open range. Presently the team was halted and the two men got out and one of them set up what appeared to be a surveying transit. It occurred to Lance that the Pendletons were having their boundaries checked.

Presently a buggy approached from the direction of Rossiter and Lance saw it leave the road and halt near the two surveyors. Lance got up and stretched and the movement must have caught the attention of one of the men, for he pointed and they all turned to look in Lance's direction. The man in the buggy immediately set the vehicle in motion, turning it and coming rapidly towards Lance.

Curious, Lance remained where he was, watching. As the vehicle drew near he noticed the fashionable attire of the driver and saw that he was wearing a brown beard. In the next moment he recognized Mark Rossiter. The buggy came to a stop close to Lance and Rossiter's cold eyes stabbed at the man in cowboy garb who so steadily returned the gaze. The banker asked sharply, "Who are you? What are you doing here?"

"Is this your range?" asked Lance.

"No, it isn't. I happen to be mayor of Rossiter and the president of the bank. I have a financial interest in the Stars and Bars and I consider it my duty to order away any trespassers I come across."

"By financial interest I suppose you mean that you've lent Colonel Pendleton money. That doesn't give you the authority to order me off the land. As a matter of fact you're trespassing yourself."

Rossiter glared at him and Lance returned the glare with interest. His meeting with the big man only intensified the dislike which had been born that night four years ago. The banker said, "You'll be hearing from me, young man," and reined the horse about and sent it trotting towards the watching surveyors.

Lance sat down on the stone again and watched. He saw Rossiter speak to the surveyors, saw them get back into the buckboard and drive away, saw Rossiter follow them into town. After a while he saw two horsemen come from town and ride towards him. He moved quickly to the protection of the trees where he could watch without being seen.

The horsemen struck the fringe of trees a hundred yards or so below him and rode slowly along the creek, their eyes probing the spaces in search of his camp. Lance felt the hair at the back of his neck prickle. One of the horsemen was Dave Schultz.

They came quite close to the tree behind which he stood and he heard Schultz exclaim. "There it is!" The horses were reined in among the trees and headed towards the camp. Schultz drew his Colt, his gaze fastened on the blanket roll beside the low fire.

When they had passed, Lance stepped quietly from behind the tree and followed them, and he too had drawn his gun. They halted near the fire and sat looking about them, then Schultz said, "Gone after his hoss, likely. Keep your eyes open, Pete." He swung from the saddle, walked to the blanket roll and started to unstrap it.

Lance said, "Don't do it, Schultz."

The marshal straightened swiftly and wheeled. He saw the levelled Colt and did not raise his gun. The man who had remained on his horse snapped his head around to stare. Lance said, "Looks like I caught a pair of thieves in the act." Schultz made an angry gesture. "Thieves my eye! You know I'm the Marshal of Rossiter. I rode out here to order you off the Stars and Bars range."

"As town marshal you have no authority here. You ought to know that. Now get on your horse and clear out of here before I get mad."

Schultz stood glaring at him and Lance eyed him steadily, keeping his Colt levelled. He repeated, "I said to get on your horse and clear out."

Schultz thrust his gun into its holster, swung

into the saddle and said, "Come on, Pete; we'll get this bird all the authority he wants."

They rode past Lance and out on the range, but instead of turning towards Rossiter they swung left and set off up the valley at a high lope.

Lance holstered his gun and caught up his horse. He knew what the next move would be and could find no way to counter it; but he wouldn't leave until the orders came from the proper source.

They came within the next two hours. He had saddled up and was seated on the rock with his horse standing by when he saw a body of riders coming down the valley and presently recognized Schultz and his companion among them. They rode up to where Lance sat and halted, and a lean, hard-bitten man said, "I'm Buck Borden, foreman of the Stars and Bars and actin' for Colonel Pendleton durin' his absence. You're trespassin' on our range and I'm orderin' you off. If you don't go peaceably we'll ride you off, and it'll be on a rail instead of a hoss."

Lance nodded. "I prefer the horse." He got up and looked them over slowly, letting his gaze fasten on each man in turn as though to stamp their features on his memory. "It's the first time I ever heard of a man being run off a cow range for making camp there. I'll remember the breach of courtesy and return it someday."

He mounted his horse, gave them a final

glance, then headed slowly for the road and Rossiter. He had gone only a short distance when he heard hoofbeats behind him. He reined off the road and sat his horse, his hand on the butt of his Colt while Schultz and his companion rode by. When they had passed he swung back into the trail and once more made for the town.

He rode to the hotel, dismounted and tied his horse, a little grin of anticipation on his lips. He thought he knew what was coming but wanted to give the owner of the Taylor House every break. He went into the lobby and crossed to the desk. The clerk gave him a cold glance and Lance recognized Edward Taylor. Lance said, "I was registered here the other day. I'd like the same room back."

Edward said, "There are no rooms available."

Lance raised his eyebrows. "You don't say! How about a cot somewhere where I won't be in the way?"

Edward looked down his nose at him. "This is a hotel, not a flophouse."

"So Dave Schultz beat me to it, eh?"

"I don't know what you're talking about," said Edward stiffly, but Lance knew by the flush which came into his cheeks that he did.

"It doesn't matter," said Lance. "I can probably find room somewhere on the public domain. I think I'd prefer it, the air's much cleaner."

He went outside and mounted his horse with

the intention of seeking a camping place where he would not be molested, but as he rode by Abner Stacy's cabin Abner himself came trotting out and halted him. "Come in, come in!" he invited, "I'm just fixin' to start supper and you're gonna eat with me."

Lance grinned down at him. "Sorry, Abner, but I'm *persona non grata* at the moment. For some reason your town marshal doesn't like me and he tipped off the hotel to say they were full up when I asked for a room."

"I don't care what kind of a *persona* you are," said Abner angrily. "You git off that hoss and come in. I got lots of room."

"You're apt to get into trouble for sheltering me."

Abner glared. "When the time comes that I can't have a friend in my own home I'll oil up my sixgun and go skunk huntin'!"

Lance's grin widened. "Thanks, oldtimer. There seem to be quite a few skunks in Rossiter; maybe you and I can have some fun deodorizing them."

He rode around the stable, put up his horse and went into the cabin.

Two

Lance remained overnight with Abner and the next morning set out for Junction City. He reached the county seat around midafternoon and an hour later Don Esteban arrived with an escort. Their business was concluded the following day and Lance, under the imposing title of the Avenger Cattle Company, came into the possession of the ancestral acres of the Guiterras family. Don Esteban would vacate the property within a month.

Lance had engaged a room at the hotel when first he had arrived from the East and had kept it because of the two trunks and other luggage he had fetched with him; now he saw to the storage of the baggage pending his occupation of Don Esteban's *hacienda*, when he would arrange for its transportation to his new home. This attended to, he rode back to Rossiter, reaching Abner's house in time for supper. Over the meal he told the old man of the purchase.

"Wal, that sure is fine!" declared Abner warmly. "I reckon it means that you'll be around yere from now on runnin' things for this Avenger Cattle Comp'ny. I cottoned to you right from the start, Lance, and I'm glad I'm gonna be seein' more of you." He looked up a bit anxiously. "You *will* be runnin' things for the comp'ny won't you?"

Lance gave him a grin. He liked Abner and felt that he could be trusted. He said, "I'm going to let you in on a little secret, Abner. I *am* the Avenger Cattle Company."

"*You!* You mean you bought out Don Esteban with your own money under that name?"

"That's right."

"Holy smokes, feller! Why—why it musta took a fortune to buy all that land and stock. Thousands and thousands of dollars."

"I guess you'd call me a pretty rich man, Abner."

Abner stared at him. "Wal, I'll be dogged! Nobody'd ever think it. I mean," he added hastily, "you ain't nothing like what I thought a feller with all that *dinero* would be like. You ain't nothin' like Mark Rossiter, for instance."

"Thank God for that!" said Lance fervently. "I was wondering whether my three and a half years in the East had spoiled me. I spent quite a bit on my education, Abner, and most of it went for something else besides what you'd call book learning. I learned to eat with a fork and I wore dress suits and fancy sportswear. I belonged to expensive clubs, smoked fifty-cent cigars, ate caviar and even attended the opera."

"My gosh!" said Abner in an awed voice. "What did you want to torture yourself thataway for?"

"I wanted to make myself superior to the Rossiter crowd. I met them four years ago, here in Mustang. I was an awkward, ignorant boy of nineteen, as poor as Job's turkey. They ridiculed me and—" He broke off. "I won't tell you about it tonight. Tomorrow, if you feel like it, we'll ride up into the hills that overlook the valley and I'll show you why I want to punish that bunch of fakers, why I want to break them, humble them. The whole crowd of them, the Pendletons included."

Abner gazed at him steadily for a full minute. Lance's face was set in harsh lines and his eyes were smouldering. He was staring across the table and it was as though he were seeing a picture of the past that shook him to the depths.

Abner finally tore his gaze away and cleared his throat noisily. He got up and fetched the bottle of Kentucky bourbon. "We need somethin' to cheer us up," he said brightly. "Try a slug of this in your coffee; it's right warmin'."

After breakfast the next morning Lance asked, "Feel like taking that ride I mentioned last night?"

"Feller, I'm all agog. Let's git goin'."

They saddled up and rode into the valley, taking the trail which paralleled the creek until they found a place where they could ford the stream. Once on the other side Lance headed for the southern range of hills. On that side of the valley he found a trail which angled upward and led the way into it.

The morning was bright and sunny but depression settled about him and seemed to grow thicker with the ascent. Four years before he had climbed this very trail and the memory of what he had found at its end returned to haunt him. After an hour's steady climb they left the trail and moved eastward through dense brush, and twenty minutes later emerged into a little clearing where a mountain brook bubbled over the stones. They halted their horses and for a short space Lance gazed about him, his eyes somber and brooding.

He spoke at last. "This is where my grandfather and I camped four years ago. He was all I had, Abner. My father and mother both died in a hotel fire when I was eight and Grandad took me and raised me. He was a prospector and I tramped the hills with him for eleven years."

He did not face Abner but spoke over the head of his horse, staring straight ahead of him.

"Hiram Jones was a kindly man and one of the world's greatest optimists. Somewhere in the hills was gold and he firmly believed that one day we were going to find it in sufficient amounts to last us the rest of our lives. But in all those eleven years we sought it together we found just enough to keep body and soul together.

"We were desperately poor. I didn't know what decent clothes were, I never knew any companionship but his. I had never been inside a schoolroom, or played with boys and girls of my age. Grandad taught me my letters and how to figure and I practiced on paper when I could get it, on slabs of wood, on the bare earth. My only textbook was an old Bible that had belonged to my mother."

He paused for a moment, his face bleak, then went on. "We camped here and prospected a little way up the brook. Grandad found signs of gold when we sank our shaft and was all excited about it. We went down to bed rock and then started a drift into the side of the hill. The sign kept getting better and he didn't want to quit work even to eat. I had to coax him away from the claim in order that he'd get nourishment and rest. He just knew that we were going to strike it this time.

"One evening I went to a little cluster of rocks overlooking the valley where I liked to sit and read the Bible before it got dark. I was sitting there when a girl came riding up the trail and walked to where I was. I didn't hear her until she spoke to me. She sat down beside me and we talked. She was a pretty thing, about sixteen years old, and she told me her name was Nancy

Pendleton and that she and her grandfather owned the big ranch on the other side of the valley.

"She was angry because a boy named Ben Clark whom she had expected to take her to a big dance in Mustang had asked Stella Rossiter instead. She was left without an escort, all the other eligible young men having made their arrangements far in advance. She sat looking at me and suddenly her eyes brightened and she asked me if I could dance. I told her that I hadn't much chance in the past but that I'd certainly like to. I guess she just took it for granted that I knew how, for she begged me to ride to Mustang the following evening and said she'd be at the hotel with her grandfather. If I asked for her there she'd dance every dance with me. She begged so hard and I was so tempted that I promised to be there. She rode away before I could change my decision.

"I went back to camp and told Grandad and he was as happy about it as I was. He condemned himself for not seeing to it that I had occasional companions of my own age and said it would do me good to mix with other boys and girls. We pretended we were part of a square-dance set and he showed me all the movements and changes he could remember. We hummed Turkey in the Straw and Golden Slippers and swung our partners and balanced all and promenaded and had a merry time."

They were still sitting their saddles. He turned his head to Abner and asked ironically, "Is this tale boring you, oldtimer?"

"Hell, no! Keep a-talkin'. You went to this dance?"

"I went. All the next day I dreamed of the fun I was going to have that night. I dug right along with Grandad but I hardly knew what I was doing. Gold sign kept getting better but it didn't interest me at all; gold meant nothing to me except the means of buying grub and a fresh shirt once in awhile. But I didn't like the way we were doing it; I kept telling Grandad that we ought to shore up the walls before we had a cave-in.

"I could hardly eat my supper, so excited I was. I scrubbed myself with water from the brook. Grandad asked me what I was going to wear and I told him I had a clean pair of Levi's and a new shirt. He said that was no fit rigging for a dance and got some clothes from his duffel bag. He had worn them when he was a young man and they were forty years out of style, but neither of us realized it, of course."

He made a swift gesture. "You can imagine what I looked like. My shoulders were too broad for the frock coat and my arms too long, and the trousers were tight and came above my ankles. I polished my old boots but they still looked worn and clumsy. And to top it off I plastered my hair down with bear grease until

I looked like a bartender. I thought that curly hair belonged to girls, you see."

Abner said, "Yeah, I see. I reckon I know what happened when you walked in on that bunch of hyenas at Rossiter."

"Yes, I guess you do. They were all there in the lobby, waiting. I think now that Nancy had bragged about me, elaborating on what a handsome and accomplished escort she was going to have. She'd naturally want to rub it in on Ben Clark and Stella Rossiter. Well, I rode our old mare, Nellie, tied her outside and left my shabby hat on the saddle. I almost ran up the steps and across the veranda I was so eager to meet Nancy and her friends. It was my first party and I'd never before had a date with a girl.

"I burst in on them and stopped, dazzled by the splendor in front of me. I remember Mark Rossiter distinctly; I thought he looked like the President of the United States. Mrs. Rossiter stared at me through her lorgnette as though I were some kind of horrible monster. I remember Ordman and I guess I'd recognize Bennett and Dunn and the Hargrave sisters if I saw them.

"But the ones I'd surely recognize are the younger ones, the boys in their tailored clothes, the girls in fluffy gowns, all ruffles and ribbons. I saw the Colonel and Nancy. I think she was the prettiest thing I'd ever laid eyes on. She took one look at me and cried, "Oh, no!" and then

44

turned and hid her face on the Colonel's shoulder.

"I remember somebody saying in a shrill voice—I think it was the Rossiter girl—'So this is your Prince Charming, Nancy! How unique!' And then I looked down at my clothes and realized how ridiculous I must have appeared to them. I was horribly ashamed and humiliated. And then Ben Clark came towards me grinning and made a brushing motion with his hands and said, 'Outside, bum!' I guess I went haywire then. I had come expecting friendship and smiles and I was met with abuse and ridicule. I leaped forward and hit Ben; hit him smack on the mouth. He went over backwards and I know I loosened his teeth.

"They all piled on me then, the Ordman boys, the Taylor boys, Tom Bennett and some of the men. I remember that Leander Taylor kept kicking me in the side after they got me down; he was furious, I guess, because I'd started a fight in his hotel. One of the women started screaming and Dave Schultz came rushing in.

"He took a couple kicks at me himself, then started untangling the pile on top of me. He snapped handcuffs on me and marched me down to the jail. I was locked in a cell and kept there overnight. The next morning Schultz and a deputy came after me. They gave me no breakfast but marched me along the street with a gun at my back and the Ordman and Taylor boys and Tom

Bennett and Ben Clark trailing along jeering and telling me what they'd do if I ever came back.

"My mare, Nellie, was still at the hitching rack. They hadn't fed or watered her. They fetched her along and at the end of the street Dave Schultz put the rein into my hand and told me to ride and not come back. And I told them that I would come back and that when I did I'd make every one of them sorry for what they had done to me.

"It was pure brag, of course. I don't know how a poor, ignorant cuss like me could have hurt them. In a few days I'd have probably forgotten my threat. But—" He broke off and wheeled his horse. "Come along, Abner; I want to show you something."

They rode along the brook for a quarter of a mile or so and then halted. At the edge of the stream was the Long Tom Lance and his grandfather had used to wash the dirt they dug. It was weatherbeaten and apparently had not been touched since Lance had left it. There were piles of tailings nearby and the mouth of the drift yawned at them from the slope of the hill.

Lance said, "This is where we were digging. On that morning I hurried back to camp realizing that Grandad would be at work and would be wondering what had happened to me. I got into my work clothes and came up here. I thought he was in the drift and went in after him. It was dark; either the lantern had gone out or had not been lit. I felt my way forward until I came to a wall of dirt and then I knew. In his eagerness to get to the gold Grandad had not taken time to shore up and the tunnel had caved in on him."

"Good gosh!" said Abner in an awed voice.

"I dug him out. It took me all day, for I had to shore up as I went along. I worked like a trooper in the hope that I would reach him in time. I found him at last; he had died instantly, crushed by the stone and earth. I dragged his poor old body out and then I collapsed. When I was able to do so I dug a grave, washed and dressed him and put him into it." He turned with a sudden fierce energy to Abner. "Can't you see? They did it! If they hadn't put me in the filthy jail and kept me there I would have been here. I would have insisted that we shore up before going any farther into that drift. But for them, Grandad would not have died! Now do you understand why I hate them—why I want to tear them down and break them?"

"Yeah, Lance, I understand."

"Come." Lance wheeled his horse and started back the way they had come. A short distance from the camp he turned off the trail and led the way to a little knoll with a solitary guardian pine beside it. On the knoll was a mound, flattened by time and covered with grass, with a roughly made cross at its head. Lance dismounted and removed his hat and for a moment stood beside it with bowed head.

Presently he turned and his face was calm again. He said to Abner quietly, "The day I put him there I promised him I'd come back and avenge him. You understand now why I called myself the Avenger Cattle Company. I don't know yet how I can hurt them, but I'll find a way."

He remounted and led the way down the trail and into the valley.

During the descent into the valley they did not exchange a word, but when finally they emerged on the open range Abner said, "I reckon I can guess the rest of the story, Lance. You found gold in that drift, didn't you?"

"Yes. There was a piece of quartz in Grandad's hand when I found him. I had to pry his fingers loose to get it out. I flung it aside without examining it. It was dark when I'd finished, I was dog tired and hadn't eaten since the evening before. I bolted some cold food and turned in.

"In the morning I missed the smell of smoke and frying bacon and realized that Grandad would never prepare another meal for me. I felt very much alone. When I'd eaten I sat down to make my plans. I didn't know what to do but I was sure I was through with prospecting.

"My father had been a ranch foreman and I'd learned to ride and rope almost as soon as I could walk. I thought I'd like to be a cattleman and decided to find a job as cowboy. I was cleaning up camp when I happened to see the chunk of quartz I'd taken out of Grandad's hand. I picked it up and looked at it more carefully. It was a very rich specimen. And then I remembered that I had no money to buy clothes or equipment and the thought came to me that perhaps I owed it to Grandad to try to find the gold for which he gave his life.

"I went back into the drift and got to work and after a while I uncovered the vein. It was a big one and before the end of the next day I knew I had struck it rich. I decided to work the claim, for money would mean a shortcut to the cattle business. And then it came to me that with money I might find a way to avenge the death of Hiram Jones. I really went to work then.

"I rode to Junction City, filed on the claim, and with the gold I had already taken out I bought another horse and a wagon and some supplies. I hauled the ore to a stamp mill and deposited the proceeds to my credit in a bank, keeping just enough cash to see me through to another load.

"I worked right through the summer and into the fall. I knew now what I was going to do. By the middle of November my bank balance was so large that it scared me. I closed the drift with blasting powder and removed all promising signs of gold from the tailings. I sold the horses and the wagon, drew a couple thousand dollars from the bank and arranged for the transfer of the balance. I outfitted myself with clothes and went to Chicago.

"I put up at a small hotel and advertised for a private tutor. I was ashamed to go to school at my age and I was in a hurry to make up for lost time. I was lucky enough to find a good teacher and I can tell you I kept him busy tossing knowledge my way. At his suggestion I put myself into the hands of a fashionable tailor and soon I was a well-dressed young man.

"I joined a gymnasium class and took boxing lessons, and I think I did it because I wanted to be ready to meet those young men who had pounded me so unmercifully that night in Mustang. I went horseback riding every Sunday just to keep my hand in. With a better command of English and the ability to wear the right kind of clothes I started branching out socially. I joined a club and soon was accepting invitations to parties. I went to art galleries and museums and I attended the opera.

"In the summers we called a halt to lessons and my teacher became my traveling companion. We visited the cities of the East and spent several weeks at a fashionable summer resort. When fall came we returned to Chicago and the lessons.

"At the end of three and a half years my teacher confessed that he had taught me everything he knew, so I paid him a bonus, packed two trunks and a couple valises and set out for Mustang. At Junction City I bought a cowboy outfit, .45 Colt, Winchester rifle, this horse and rig, and rode to Mustang to look things over. And that," he finished, "brings us up to date."

"It's an interestin' story," said Abner. "Jest like one of them novels. But I don't see how you're gonna hurt Rossiter and his bunch. If they was ranchin' you could crowd 'em out or sheep 'em out; but here in town—" He made a gesture of futility.

"All I can do now is wait. I always wanted to be a cattleman and I couldn't have found a better range; and the valley is close to town and I can keep my eye on Rossiter and his gang and be ready to take advantage of any opening they give me. And the Pendletons are ranching. Don't forget, they helped humiliate me. I'll admit Nancy was in an embarrassing position, but I always think of the king who had a country cousin to dinner. The cousin poured his tea into a saucer and sipped it and the king promptly did likewise. The rest of the guests didn't dare laugh then. That was real gentility. If she had welcomed me it wouldn't have taken me long to realize how sadly I was out of place and I would have effaced myself as gracefully as possible. But that would have been expecting too much of a proud, aristocratic Pendleton, I guess."

"Make that a high-spirited, sixteen-year-old

51

girl," corrected Abner. "You can't blame her so much; she likely had bragged you up to her high-toned friends and the letdown was just too much for a kid like her, Pendleton or no Pendleton."

"Maybe so," said Lance shortly. "But the Pendletons run with the pack of wolves in town and must take their medicine with the rest."

They returned to town and Abner insisted that Lance remain his guest until Don Esteban had given him possession of the *hacienda*. Lance readily accepted the invitation; the more he saw of Abner the more he liked him. He spent a few days moving about the town, watching the Rossiter bunch, satisfying himself that his judgment of them had been correct.

He found them arrogant and intolerant, treating the merchants with condescension and the natives with contempt. They formed a clique, giving teas and parties first at the home of one and then another. Ben Clark was the only outsider except the Pendletons whom they accepted as an equal and Lance was sure that this was due to the fact that he and his father were Northerners like themselves. Since Lance was a Southerner this did not mitigate his feelings towards them. In a sense they were fighting the Civil War all over.

Dave Schultz stalked him and Lance knew the marshal was hoping for an excuse to throw him in jail or order him out of town. Mark Rossiter was another who resented his presence. The pompous banker glared at him when they met on the street and Lance could feel his angry stare after he had passed. Undoubtedly Rossiter had given Schultz his orders to get something on Lance which would give them the excuse to banish him.

The frameup came that night, although at the time it bore none of the earmarks of one. Lance and Abner had gone into the Wildcat for a drink or two before turning in and were standing at the bar talking quietly when the man who had been with Dave Schultz the day they tried to put Lance off the Stars and Bars range entered. He appeared to be half drunk and the other customers gave him plenty of room.

Lance saw him enter and called Abner's attention to him. "Who's the surly looking brute that just came in?" he asked in a low voice.

Abner glanced in the direction Lance had indicated. "Name's Pete Paradine. Nobody knows for sure but rumor has it that he's a road agent and comes to Mustang to lay low after a job. Never seems to work but always has money to spend for hooch. Schultz uses him once in a while for strong-arm work and I've heard he's chain lightnin' on the draw. Why?"

Lance told the old man of their encounter on Stars and Bars range.

Abner looked worried. "Mebbe we'd better

clear outa here; looks like he's carryin' a load and lookin' for trouble."

"I'm not packing my gun and can use my fists with anybody. No matter how drunk he is he won't shoot an unarmed man. But we'll go when we've finished this drink."

They downed their beer and turned towards the entrance. Paradine had turned his back to the bar and was scowling at the world in general. They did not glance at him, but he saw them and as they were about to pass he growled, "Hey, you!"

They ignored him. He lunged forward suddenly and seized Lance by an arm and swung him around. "I'm talkin' to you!"

Lance held his temper in check. "What is it?"

"Pulled a gun on me the other day, didn't you?"

"No, I pulled it on Dave Schultz, who'd already pulled his and was going through my blanket roll."

"Same thing; I was with Dave. No man pulls a gun on me and then talks his way outa it."

"I'll remember that when I pull one on you."

Paradine's glance went to Lance's waist. "Where is that gun of yores? Hid it under yore arm?"

"It's hanging on a wall peg. It'd be a good time to shoot me if you can make yourself mad enough."

The man's scowl deepened. "I ain't no baby-killer. Go home and git it and come back. I'll be waitin' for you."

"You'll have a long wait. When I go home I'm going to bed."

"Yaller, huh? All right, pilgrim, I'll put it this way: you git yoreself outa town before mornin' or be ready to use it. Get me? At sunup I'll start lookin' for you and if I find you, gun or no gun, they'll carry you wherever you're goin' feet first." He released his grip on Lance's arm and backed to the bar. His lips were curled in a malignant sneer.

Lance said, "See you later, then," and walked to the door and outside.

Abner said worriedly, "Now you're in for it. You'd better git out."

"No. If it's a frameup, damned if I'll give them the satisfaction of getting away with it. Let's look for Dave Schultz; as town marshal he's bound to stop a shootout here in town."

They searched for Dave and did not find him; nobody had seen him since suppertime.

"That settles it," said Lance grimly. "It's a frameup, all right. Abner, where can I get a good sleeve gun?"

"Prob'ly at Hank Wetherby's store; but what you want with a thing like that? You been ordered outa town and you got the right to defend yourself any way you want to, but you gotta straighten your arm to get a sleeve gun into your hand and you can yank a belt gun just as quick. Only thing a sleeve gun's good for is to take somebody by su'prize."

"That's just what I hope to do." He gave Abner

a gold coin. "Slip up to the store and buy one for me. And fetch along a left-handed holster while you're at it."

He went on to the cabin and Abner rejoined him there within twenty minutes.

"Here you are; sleeve gun and ammunition for it and a left-handed holster. What in time is that for? You ain't left-handed."

"Pete Paradine doesn't know that. If he noticed that I had my gun in my right hand the other day he'll be a little confused."

He rigged the sleeve gun and practiced letting it slide into his hand. He worked at it for an hour before he was sure of his dexterity, then grinned cheerfully at Abner. "I feel better now. It'll work."

"What's the idee of a left-handed holster? You ain't practiced drawin' with your left hand."

"I don't have to practice." He told Abner why and the old man let a slow grin spread across his face. "Wal, I'll be goldarned!" he said.

They turned in then and both slept well.

They were up at dawn and had their breakfast. The sun was just above the horizon when Lance said, "Abner, take a look around town for Dave Schultz. My money says he isn't present, but we'll make sure."

Abner returned within half an hour. "Dave ain't in town. Somebody said he rode out to the Stars and Bars last night to see Buck Borden.

And Pete Paradine's struttin' up and down the street boastin' of what he's gonna do to you if you show up."

Lance nodded and reached for his gunbelt. He had attached the left-handed holster with the .45 Colt in it, and now he buckled it about him. He put on his coat, rigged the sleeve gun and practiced a few times to be sure it would not catch in the lining. He said, "Take a look and tell me when Paradine's at the other end of the street."

Abner went outside and came in at once. "He's up in front of the hotel and they's a gang gatherin' on both sides of the street."

"Keno! Here I go." Lance put a sealed envelope into Abner's hand. "Just in case I've guessed wrong," he said. "If I come back alive we'll tear it up."

Abner wrung his hand. "Good luck, feller!"

Lance stepped out into the street, walked to its middle and headed towards the hotel. An excited shout went up at sight of him and Paradine stared hard for a moment then came towards him rapidly, almost eagerly.

Lance moved ahead steadily, the dust squirting from his boots. The distance between them diminished rapidly. Lance's right arm was crooked, the hand grasping the lapel of his coat; at his left hip swung the Colt and he kept his left hand eight or ten inches from the butt,

57

fingers curved in preparation for the draw. Only he didn't intend to draw.

There was sixty feet of dusty road between them now. Lance let his right hand fall naturally to his side, felt the comforting feel of the little gun slide into his palm. The gun was cocked and his finger was ready to curl about the trigger. Paradine was watching his left hand, which was just what he wanted him to do.

On both sidewalks men were walking along with him, and more men were advancing with Paradine. Lance made no move for the gun at his hip, hoping that a gunman of Paradine's prowess would scorn to draw until he made a move. The distance had dwindled to forty feet—to thirty. They weren't close enough yet for Lance to be sure. Paradine kept his gaze fixed on Lance's left hand, his own gun hand ready to swoop and pull. Twenty feet. Lance caught the barest possible flicker of Paradine's eyes, saw the almost imperceptible tightening of his lips.

Lance made a stab at his left hand, saw Paradine start like lightning for his own gun. Lance raised his right arm, aimed and pulled the trigger of the sleeve gun. It was so close that he could not miss. He saw the dust spurt from Paradine's vest where the bullet struck him, beneath the right shoulder, just where he had aimed.

The heavy slug threw Paradine off balance, whirled him around to the right. The gun had cleared its holster but the strength had gone from his arm and he could not raise it. His fingers opened and the Colt fell into the dusty street. Then Paradine fell on top of it.

He was not dead; Lance, having tricked the man, did not want to go that far. But the bullet had nicked the top of the lung and Paradine was due for a long stay in bed.

Lance turned around and went home.

The next day Lance rode into the valley, ostensibly to pay a visit to Don Esteban, in reality to look over more carefully the range which was now his. He rode slowly up the trail and reached the *hacienda* around the middle of the afternoon. Don Esteban insisted that he remain for the evening meal and afterwards urged him to stay overnight; but Lance said he would enjoy the ride back in the moonlight and set out after they had gone through the lengthy ritual of farewell. It was a mild night with a gentle breeze blowing and he rode slowly, following the course of the creek.

He was half way down the valley when his horse stopped and cocked inquiring ears. In the silence Lance heard the sound of plodding hoofs and saw approaching along the creek a mass which he identified as a small bunch of cattle. He quickly reined into the shadow of the trees and sat his horse, watching. Cattle being driven at night usually meant but one thing.

The mass came slowly ahead and he could see a horseman riding point and a couple more on the flanks. The point man reined towards the creek and the flankers came racing up to turn the cattle. The animals moved into a gap in the trees beyond which Lance guessed was a ford. He heard the splashing of water and knew his guess was correct. The animals were being driven to the far side of the creek. One of the flankers crossed with them and the other remained where he was, turning the column. Presently a drag rider came into sight and the second flanker crossed with him. With the cattle had gone two more riders who would guard the other flank when in the open.

The moonlight was bright but held that hazy quality which obscures details; Lance could see both men and animals, but the features of the former and the markings on the latter were indistinguishable. He counted some fifty steers and six riders.

Rustling? Looked very much like it. If so, it was probably Stars and Bars stock which was being stolen. Well, let them go to it; they could steal the Pendletons blind for all he cared.

At the breakfast table the next morning he said, "Abner, this son of yours down in Texas; think he'd take the job of foreman of my ranch?"

Abner's eyes kindled. "Lance, he's just the feller for you! Big and strong and knows cows from the horns down. I'll write him right away."

"Tell me where he is and I'll deliver the letter in person. Don Esteban won't be pulling out for a month. If your boy accepts my proposition we can gather a crew while I'm waiting; and if he does the job the way I want it done, I'll set him up in business for himself when the thing's over."

"He's mighty proud, Lance; he wouldn't let me set him up and I'm his own father."

"We'll make it part of agreement. I'll pay him so much a month and tack the land and cows on as a bonus."

So it came about that the very same morning saw Lance headed towards Texas bearing a letter from Abner to his son, Joe Stacy. A week and five hundred miles later he was talking it over with Joe. He liked the young man at once; Joe was tall and lean and hard-faced and there could be no doubt of his ability.

When Lance had made his offer Joe said, "There's just one thing to say to an offer of that kind, Mr. Jones. It sounds so good that if it wasn't for Pop's letter I'd be suspicious, but he says it's all right and his judgment is good enough for me. I'll take the job. My boss knows I'm aiming to quit as soon as I find me a place to start a ranch, so he won't be hurt none. We can round up a crew and be in the valley by the time the Don's ready to get out."

They shook hands on it, Joe gave notice to his

boss, and for the next two weeks they traveled around recruiting a crew. They picked one man here, another there, until they had a dozen good, tough, dependable men. Joe knew them all and vouched for them. Lance told Joe of his plan of vengeance but the crew was kept in ignorance. They were primarily for the purpose of working cattle but would be capable of defending their owner's property if the Pendleton's tough crew didn't like the medicine Lance intended to dish out.

At the end of the second week they gathered their men and started on the five-hundred-mile return trip. They entered the valley from the west, thus avoiding Rossiter, and found Don Esteban ready to move. Guiterras sent his *vaqueros* on with the loaded freighting wagons and the next day he himself departed with his retinue. The new crew immediately took over and started a roundup of cattle for the purpose of taking a tally.

Lance gave Joe his instructions that evening. "For the present I don't want my connection with the Avenger Cattle Company known even to the crew. I'm simply acting as their agent. You'll handle things just as though the ranch were yours. Go to the county seat and register our brand in the name of the company. It will be an A with a C attached to each leg of the A. Take a wagon and load up with enough wire to fence clear across the valley. When the men have finished tallying, we'll put them to cutting posts. The day of free range is over so far as the Clarks and Pendletons are concerned."

Joe nodded, studying him. Lance's face was set in firm lines. He owed the Clarks and Pendletons nothing but animosity and was prepared to dish it out aplenty. Joe did not blame him; he judged Lance to be friendly and generous but he also judged him to be a loyal man and grateful to old Hiram Jones for taking him and caring for him when he had been orphaned. But for these people and their Yankee friends, old Hiram might have lived.

Lance rode into Rossiter the next morning to find the town decked out in flags and bunting and, knowing the day was not a holiday, wondered about it. He reined in his horse and sat looking about him, and then Marshal Dave Schultz stepped out of his office and glared at him. Schultz said, "I thought we'd got rid of you."

"No such luck, my worthy minion of the law. What's going on here? Old man Rossiter celebrating a birthday?"

"Don't be so danged smart. And keep your nose clean while you're in town."

"You'd like to catch me without a handkerchief sometime, wouldn't you?" He grinned at the glowering marshal and rode on to Abner's cabin. He went around to the back and was stabling his horse when the old man came popping in.

"How'd you make out, feller?"

"Fine. Joe's out on the ranch with a dozen fighting Texans. He said to tell you that he'll pay you a visit as soon as he gets straightened out."

"You got back jest in time for the doin's. Mebbe you noticed the decorations. Nancy Pendleton's comin' home today. Ben Clark drove to Junction City to fetch her and the Colonel. They'll put up at the hotel and there's gonna be a big homecomin' banquet and dance. Reg'lar Queen of Sheby, she is."

Lance witnessed the homecoming that evening. He had gone to the store to buy some tobacco and had just been waited on when somebody yelled, "Here they come!" and there was a concerted rush for the door. Lance went with the others and stood on the porch looking up the street. Approaching at a sedate walk was a team of fine horses drawing a double buckboard. Two men sat on the front seat and when they drew nearer Lance recognized Ben Clark as one of them. The white hair and goatee identified the Colonel as one of the passengers in the rear seat; of Nancy, Lance could glimpse just a bit of poke bonnet, a few tantalizing curls and part of a shoulder.

Knowing that they would stop at the hotel, he crossed the street and joined the throng waiting there. Mayor Rossiter stood at the foot of the steps; he was faultlessly dressed and carried his gold headed cane. Behind him on the hotel veranda were grouped the other social lights of Rossiter. Common citizens stood at the respectful distance on either side of the mayor and Dave Schultz saw to it that a lane to the veranda was kept clear. Lance slipped through the crowd to a place in its front rank just four or five feet from the pompous Rossiter.

The buckboard drew up at the edge of the sidewalk and Ben handed the reins to the man who rode with him, vaulted over the wheel and extended a hand. Nancy, bright-eyed and smiling, took the hand and stepped lightly to the ground.

Lance caught his breath. Four years had done things to Nancy and all for the best. He remembered her as graceful and lovely, but now the slimness, while still there, was a bit more softly rounded, the beauty that of a young woman rather than that of a sixteen-year-old girl. He hardly noticed the Colonel as he stepped with quiet dignity from the vehicle and gave his granddaughter his arm.

Mayor Rossiter removed his beaver hat with a flourish, cocked it over an arm and bowed over the hand Nancy extended to him He said, "Welcome home, Nancy. Welcome to Rossiter." He just had to get in the name.

She smiled, her violet eyes dancing. "It's so nice to be back, Mr. Rossiter. And how lovely you've made the old town!" She glanced up at the group on the veranda and waved at the Bennetts, the Ordmans, the Dunns and the Taylors. She even smiled warmly at Stella Rossiter and her mother. The two Hargrave sisters fluttered their handkerchiefs at her.

She moved forward, her pleased glances going to the grinning natives on both sides. And suddenly she stopped short and Lance saw her eyes widen. She was staring directly at him.

He stood tall and erect, his hat pushed back on his curly dark hair and stared back at her frankly but with no hint of recognition in his eyes. He saw the flush leave her face, saw her lips part slightly as though they were about to utter his name. In that brief moment she had recognized the boy she had last seen here at this hotel over four years ago. Or thought she had. The next instant she was just as sure she had been mistaken; there was no responsive light in the dark eyes, they were those of an utter stranger.

The Colonel had halted with her and was looking down at her inquiringly. She removed her gaze and the flush returned to her cheeks. She moved on and ascended the veranda steps and was immediately surrounded by her friends.

Lance moved along the street, a cynical smile twisting his lips. She was still the Lady Bountiful, still the proud Pendleton. Pride, he was telling himself, cometh before a fall.

Three

The next few minutes were spent by Nancy in a flurry of polite handshaking, bows and curtsies and pecks on the cheeks, in replying to speeches of congratulation and anxious inquiries as to the state of her health after the tiring trip from Louisville. It wasn't until she had reached the sanctuary of her room that she had time to think of the stranger who had so closely resembled Lancelot Jones.

It just couldn't be Lance; this man was broader and fuller in the face than Lance. Still four years would make a lot of difference. Four years; that would make him twenty-three. No, this couldn't be Lance Jones; this man looked older. Twenty-five or twenty-six. He had dark curly hair and blue eyes with heavy lashes, but there the resemblance ended. He wore much better clothes than poor Lance could afford and he wore them with the assurance of a man who is used to them. But she would have to ask about this dark, handsome stranger just to set her mind at rest.

Lance at the moment had just entered the cabin to find Abner rocking and smoking. The old fellow's eyes twinkled as he asked, "You been on the reception committee?"

"I saw her arrive. She came in state with driver and footman. They bowed and curtsied all over the place. I was at the front of the crowd and she saw me and thought she recognized me. I looked right through her and I guess she decided I couldn't possibly be that wretched Lancelot Jones." He tossed his hat on a chair and sat down. "I think we ought to go to the dance tonight."

"And git tossed out on our ears!"

"No, it's going to be a public affair. Miss Nancy Pendleton belongs to the town tonight. Everybody in Rossiter is welcome and she'll dance with anybody who asks her."

"You gonna dance with her?"

"Not so's you'd notice it. I'd like to be the only one who doesn't."

"I'd like to see that."

"Then you'll go?"

"Yeah, I'll tag along."

Lance prepared carefully for the dance. The clothes he had brought from the East were in storage at Junction City, but those he wore were excellently tailored and would never go out of style in cow country. He pressed the coat and trousers and polished the black Spanish leather boots until they shone like mirrors. He put on an expensive white silk shirt and a blue silk scarf.

Abner said, "You sure look like that Beau

68

Brummel feller. The gals are gonna fall over themselves tryin' to dance with you."

They walked to the hotel together, arriving around eight o'clock. Rossiter's upper crust had gathered in the lobby just as they had on that other occasion. Lance and Abner took places against the wall at one side of the entrance and he knew that the Rossiters, the Bennetts, the Dunns and the Taylors and the Ordmans were observing him closely. He caught the flash of Mrs. Rossiter's lorgnette and it amused him.

He looked about him calmly, interestedly. He noticed that the clothing they wore, while stylish at the time of their arrival in Rossiter, was now outmoded in cut and fabric. It wasn't so bad with the women but some of the younger men had outgrown their coats and trousers and the ruffled shirts were beginning to show signs of wear.

Dave Schultz had dressed up for the occasion. He wore a frock coat a couple sizes too large for him and had donned his hardware beneath it. His badge had been polished and he was wearing a new black Stetson hat. He came up to Lance and stood for a moment regarding him. "Some fancy boy, ain't you?" he sneered.

"You're not so bad yourself," observed Lance pleasantly. "The coat doesn't fit and you forgot to wash your face but otherwise you cut quite a figure."

69

Dave's cheeks reddened. "Don't be so danged smart, feller." He turned away and sauntered about the lobby, but presently Lance saw him duck into the wash room and when he emerged the smudge of dust on his nose had been removed. The coat still didn't fit but there was nothing he could do about that. And then Nancy and the Colonel came down the stairs.

Again Lance felt the breathtaking impact of her beauty. Fresh and smiling and poised, she moved gracefully down the steps, a hand resting lightly on the Colonel's arm. Her gown was what they called a creation and she wore it like a queen; her violet eyes glowed and the brown curls glistened in the light from the chandelier. The crowd surged forward to greet them anew and there was a minute or two of bowing and scraping.

From within the dining room came the twang of guitars and the scrape of violins. The orchestra was tuning up. Mark Rossiter's unctuous voice said, "The grand march, ladies and gentlemen."

They formed quickly, Rossiter offering his arm to Nancy and taking the lead. The Colonel followed with Mrs. Rossiter; the lesser lights paired off and fell in behind them. The orchestra struck up a march and the column moved sedately into the ball room.

And now from outside came trooping the peasantry, merchants and their wives and sons and daughters, gamblers from the saloons, a smattering of honkytonk girls, gaudily dressed and well powdered and rouged. They followed the marchers into the room and moved to the chairs arranged along the walls. The procession had circled the room once and the leaders passed Lance and Abner just as they were about to sit down.

Lance had removed his hat and stood erect, watching. He did not let his gaze rest on Nancy more than a moment, but he was watching her just the same, and saw that little puzzled frown as she probed him with her eyes. Then she was smiling again and had passed him.

Lance could not but notice that even on such a democratic occasion the socialites intended to keep strictly to themselves. Seats at the far end of the hall had been reserved for them and the men got in each other's way in their efforts to see the ladies properly seated. There was much ado about dusting chairs and arranging them and making the girls comfortable.

Abner whispered, "I wisht I was behind old lady Rossiter's chair. I'd yank it out from under her jest as she was about to squat. She'd shore look ridiculous floppin' around on the floor like a baby rhinoceros, wouldn't she?"

Lance grinned. "You'd certainly upset her equanimity."

"Upset it! Hell, I'd turn it upside down and

tromp on it!" The orchestra struck up a waltz. Instantly the men were on their feet bowing before the ladies they had escorted. Nancy was borne away by Mark Rossiter. He danced heavily, mechanically, like a huge brown bear. The Colonel skillfully piloted the ponderous Mrs. Rossiter about the floor, managing to look dignified even in such a situation. The young men paired off with the girls. There were just twelve men and twelve women, including the Hargrave sisters. The commoners did not dance.

When the number had ended, Mayor Rossiter walked to the center of the floor. He smiled benignly on the watchers and said, "Now, folks, you must all join in the festivities. Miss Pendleton is one of you and it is in her honor that we are here. Everybody dance and have a good time."

There was a Virginia Reel then, and once more the two dozen of the elite went through the figures without help from the onlookers. Rossiter had tried to form a set from those in the chairs against the walls but was unsuccessful. He looked a bit annoyed.

Lance said to Abner, "Too bad to let Miss Pendleton down like this. Who is that dark eyed little beauty sitting over there with the girls?"

"They're honkytonk gals," said Abner, "and she's Lolita. She dances and hustles drinks down at the Wildcat Saloon."

"I think I'd like to dance with her."

Abner looked shocked. "And disgrace yourself?"

"Why not? How about introducing me?"

"To her? Hell, jest go over and ask her. She ain't bashful." The orchestra struck up another waltz. Lance walked across the floor directly to the dark eyed girl and he knew that the Rossiter crowd was watching him. Lolita looked up inquiringly and he bowed and said, "Would the *Señorita* be kind enough to dance with me?"

She looked surprised but he saw her eyes brighten. She got up promptly. "But *sí, Señor.* I weel be 'appy."

She was a pretty little thing, vivid and vibrant, slim of waist and ankle, and the bright colors she wore went well with her dark beauty. They glided out upon the floor and Lance knew at once that he had picked a winner. The eyes of the spectators were fixed on them.

They moved gracefully, Lolita anticipating his every movement, laughing in sheer enjoyment and looking up into his face. He was aware of the stares of other couples as they swept by, caught an occasional whispered, "Who is he?" Once he came out of a turn to look squarely into a pair of puzzled violet eyes; he let his gaze go past Nancy as though he had not seen her, then bent his head to whisper to Lolita, "You're a sweet little partner, *Señorita.* I bet you know all the Mexican dances."

73

"Oh, but *sí*! I dance them all, but so long ago. Sometimes I am 'omesick."

"Well, we're going to dance one tonight, *chiquita*. We're going to steal the show right away from these stuffed shirts. Game?"

The dark eyes sparkled. "Game? Oh, *sí*! Eet would make me 'appy."

The dance ended and this time there was applause from the chairs along the wall. Lance had maneuvered Lolita so that they had halted near the Mexican orchestra and the musicians were grinning at them. Lance said to the leader, "How about La Paloma?"

The man nodded vigorously and spoke to his mates. The dreamy strains of the song came whispering from guitars and mandolins. He turned to Lolita and they went into the dance, the girl snapping her fingers where the rhythm called for castanets.

It was a beautiful performance, and when they had finished there was an outburst of applause in which even the socialites joined. They did it half-heartedly except Nancy; her eyes were shining and he heard her call softly, "Oh, beautiful! Beautiful!"

It took some of the triumph away, and at the same time warmed Lance strangely. He saw Lolita back to her chair, thanked her and went over to sit beside Abner. The old fellow's eyes were twinkling. "Feller, that was what I call

74

dancin'. You made the rest of 'em look like monkeys."

He did not dance again and a sort of apathy settled over the crowd. The socialites tried their best to make things merry, but it was no go. Around ten o'clock Lance politely stifled a yawn. "Feel like absorbing more of this, or shall we go home and kill a quart?" he asked Abner.

Abner promptly stood up. "We'll dance the fandango with John Barleycorn."

They started for the doorway but before they reached it Lance saw Ben Clark coming hastily towards them. Ben caught up with them and grabbed Lance by an arm. "Wait a minute!" he said sharply. "Miss Pendleton wants to dance with you. I'm to introduce you to her; what's your name?"

"Sorry," drawled Lance. "Convey my regrets to Miss Pendleton and tell her I have an urgent appointment with the King of Siam."

Ben's face flushed and his grip tightened. "That's an insult!"

"You catch on quick. Take your hand off my arm."

Ben removed the hand but continued to glare. "I demand an apology for that insult to Miss Pendleton."

"Keep on demanding it if it makes you feel better," said Lance, and turned away.

They went through the lobby and had just

descended the steps to the street when a trio of young men came hurrying down behind them. They were Ben Clark and the two Taylor boys, George and Edward. Lance turned to face them. He could not see their faces distinctly but their intention was plain. He asked, "You gentlemen wish to speak to me?"

"You're damned right we do!" said Ben in a choked voice. "You can't get away without apologizing for that insolent message to Miss Pendleton."

"And if I refuse to apologize I suppose you intend to beat me up like you would a—bum. Well, three of you working together might manage to do it."

"We don't have to gang up on you," said Clark angrily. "One of us is plenty."

"As gentlemen," said Lance drily, "you surely wouldn't want to create a disturbance here in the street. Or does it matter?"

"We'll go around to the alley. And don't try to run away."

"I wouldn't dream of it," said Lance, and immediately moved to the corner of the hotel and rounded it. Abner hurrying along at his side. The old man was muttering to himself and Lance said in a low voice, "Keep out of it, old-timer; I'll take care of things." He removed his scarf, folded it and put it into a coat pocket, then shrugged out of the coat and handed it to Abner.

76

Light streamed from the kitchen windows in the rear of the hotel and there was a lighted lantern hanging in the doorway of the barn. Lance turned to the three who followed him and asked, "Who's first?"

"I am," said Clark, and came forward, swinging.

And now Lance reaped the reward of hours of practice with a sparring partner. He had skill and speed and he made Ben look foolish within the first minute. The big fellow made bull-like charges which he sidestepped or stooped with sharp left jabs to the nose and mouth; he dodged the wild swings or deflected them with a forearm. And finally, when he had Ben puffing and panting with exertion; he feinted with his left, drew down the clumsy guard and planted a hard right on the point of Ben's chin. Ben went down like a log.

"Next!" said Lance. He wasn't even breathing hard.

The Taylor brothers hesitated but *noblesse oblige* drove Edward into the fray. He advanced cautiously, putting up a guard which Lance found easy to penetrate. He circled the young man, stinging him with jabs, landing short, punishing punches to cheek and nose and mouth. He finally sunk a right just under Edward's breast bone and the fellow caved, hands on his stomach, chin outthrust. It made a beautiful target but Lance scorned to hit him again. He said, "You're through," and turned to George. "Want some of the same?"

George remained where he was, saying nothing. Edward staggered away like a small boy with the bellyache and sat down on the watering trough. Lance said to George, "Splash some water on Ben and wake him up," and reached for his coat. He shrugged into it while George went to the trough and dipped a handkerchief into the water. When Lance and Abner started for the street George was kneeling beside the still unconscious Ben Clark.

Abner was chuckling excitedly as they strode towards the cabin. He cackled, "Feller, you got a heap of revenge outa them last ten minutes! Turned down the great Nancy Pendleton and polished off two of her admirers. And made a third one back peddle until he set his feet afire! The tail-twistin' has begun! Let's git goin'; we still got a quart to kill."

They didn't kill the quart, but the contents of the bottle had diminished appreciably. They talked, and Lance told of his intention of fencing off his range.

"That'll sure put a crimp in the Clarks and the Pendletons," said Abner. "I sorta hate to see Nancy git hurt because she's really a fine gal. But she's bad spoilt and needs a lesson. As for the Clarks, you can't do enough to them to make me mad. That Ben is a moocher if ever I see one and sure needs takin' down a few pegs. The rest of 'em—well, I don't rightly see how you're gonna hurt them and they're the ones that you oughta git square with. They need the starch taken outa them fer a fact."

"They're all a bunch of fakirs," said Lance tightly. "I've hung around town just in order to confirm my opinion of them. They probably came out here because they couldn't make a go of it in the East. All but Rossiter. I don't know what brought him to a little cowtown like this, but I'll bet he's playing a game of some kind, a game which will pay huge profits."

They were silent for a moment, then Lance went on. "Right now I'm wondering how tonight's fight is going to turn out. I've been expecting some kind of frameup ever since I came back and now they can cook up something to hang on me."

His expectations were realized the next morning. They were cleaning up the breakfast dishes when somebody tried the front door, found it barred and pounded heavily upon it. Dave Schultz called, "Open up! It's the law."

Lance dried his hands swiftly and reached for his cartridge belt. He buckled it about him and whispered, "I'll slip out the back way. Tell him I'm not here." He snatched up his hat and walked quietly to the back door, glanced through a window to assure himself that there was nobody to stop him and went out as Abner moved towards the source of the pounding.

He rounded the house and looked around the front corner. Abner had opened the door and Dave had pushed by him. Lance heard Abner's angry voice, "What in time you mean by bustin' into my house? I told you Jones went out the back way."

"I aim to see about that."

"You got a warrant for him?"

"I don't need no warrant."

Lance ran along the front of the cabin, drew his gun and stepped across the threshold. He said, "Looking for me, Dave?" and nudged the marshal with the muzzle of the Colt.

Dave stiffened, started to wheel and thought better of it. He said, "Put that gun away. You're under arrest."

"For what?"

"Assault and battery. Judge Ordman sent me to pick you up."

"Judge? Since when?"

Schultz made an impatient gesture. "Justice of the Peace, then."

"Let's go down and see him. You first."

He moved back and Schultz turned to glare at him. Lance met the glare with one of his own and kept the Colt levelled. "I said you first."

Schultz came through the doorway and Lance

80

fell in behind him. Dave's face was red. "I ain't goin' this way; it's me that's makin' the arrest."

"This is the way we're going just the same. Start walking."

Dave strode angrily along the street, Lance a pace behind him. Schultz strode into Ordman's office and Lance heard Mark Rossiter say, "Where is he?"

"Right here," said Lance, and stepped into the room behind Schultz. He kicked the door shut and put his back against it. Schultz had halted and Lance reached out and plucked the gun from his holster. "Sit down, Dave. I'll take care of this." Schultz cursed and strode to a chair.

There were four men in the room besides Lance and the marshal; Rossiter, Ordman, Taylor and Bennett. They stared at Lance and consternation showed on their faces. Lance looked at Ordman and asked, "You wished to see me?"

The lawyer made a quick recovery. "I did. Jones, put up that gun. You're here to be tried for assault and battery."

"Yes? Who's the complainant? Where are the witnesses?"

"The complainant is suffering from the beating you gave him; we do not need witnesses, his condition speaks for itself."

Lance gave him a contemptuous look. "You're supposed to be a lawyer; you should know better

81

than that. This is simply a frameup and if you try to put it over I'll take the case to a real court and make you look foolish."

Rossiter said heatedly, "You've been a source of trouble ever since you came to Rossiter. Last night you insulted Miss Pendleton and when Ben Clark protested, as any gentleman would, you assaulted him. We don't want you around here, Jones. I'm the mayor and these gentlemen are members of the council; it is our unanimous opinion that you are a menace to the peace. We will dispense with a trial; we're simply ordering you out of Rossiter." He turned to Schultz. "Marshal, if this man is not out of town by noon, use your judgment. Arrest him, but don't run any chances. Do I make myself clear?"

"You're danged tootin' you do!" growled Dave, and Lance had no doubt what his judgment would be.

Lance smiled thinly. "I'm quite willing to leave town. But I'm leaving because I want to, because it'd be a pleasure, and because I'd intended leaving in any event. And if you—" he spoke to Schultz—"ever decide to take a potshot at me, I'll fill you so full of lead that it'll take six men and a couple of horses to drag your carcass to the cemetery."

He turned back to the others. "As for you cheap tinhorns, don't think for a moment that I'm not wise to you or that I won't drag you from your high places and put you where you belong. Do I make *myself* clear?"

They did not answer, each wondering with a feeling of panic what he had meant by saying that he was wise to them. Lance reached behind him and opened the door, then spoke to Schultz. "There's a watering trough outside the hotel; you'll find your gun in it." He went out and closed the door behind him.

There was silence in the room for a moment, then Schultz got up and strode to the door. "I'll fix that jigger good and proper," he threatened and went out.

Taylor said, "What did he mean when he said he was wise to us?"

"That's what I'm wondering," said Mark Rossiter. "It would seem that one of us has failed to keep the secret of the Rossiter Development Company."

"Not me," said Taylor positively.

Ordman shook his head.

Bennett said, "I haven't told a soul. How about you, Mark?"

Rossiter swelled up. "As a banker I'm quite used to keeping confidences." He got up and paced the room, head bowed, hands clasped behind him. It was a favorite pose; he liked to believe he looked like Napoleon. At the end of the second turn he stopped and faced them. "This man Jones; he's no common cowhand.

His clothes are tailor-made and he speaks the King's English. And I caught him watching our surveyors."

"He must know something," said Taylor uneasily.

"Personally I think he's a spy of some kind. Some company in the East might have seen our advertisements and sent him out here to look around."

"Why?" asked Ordman.

"To see if there's a boom on in the hope of getting in on the ground floor."

They thought that over. Ordman said, "Perhaps he was sent out by some prospective investors to look the situation over."

"He said," blurted Rossiter, "that he was wise to us and would drag us from our high places. Just as though we were criminals. We're not; everything we're doing or intend to do is within the law."

Ordman asked, "Taylor, are you sure that nobody but you and Mark have seen the correspondence addressed to the company?"

"Positive," answered Taylor. "The mail comes from Junction City once a week. I have the key to the mail pouches and I sort the stuff myself. The first thing I do is wrap the company mail in a separate parcel, and I deliver it to Mark in person."

"How about outgoing mail? The company's return address is on the envelopes."

Rossiter answered. "I answer the mail myself and deliver it to Leander. The correspondence is locked in my safe where nobody can get at it."

"And I lock the answers in my safe until time to put them into the pouch," said Taylor.

"I see. Now the stationery is printed in the East and I suppose you keep it out of sight."

"Of course," answered Rossiter stiffly. "It is locked in my safe. The explanation must be the one you gave, Jacob; Jones has been sent out here by prospective purchasers."

"Then the question before the meeting is what to do about Jones. If he starts talking, the whole scheme will be dragged out into the open."

Rossiter sat down. He was frowning in thought. "In that case we will have to explain that we are merely trying to ascertain in advance whether there would be sufficient responses to justify our entering into negotiations for the purchase of the necessary land." His face brightened. "Yes, that is the solution. Naturally we'd keep the matter secret for fear that the Colonel will set too high a value on the land when he learns what we want it for."

Ordman nodded. "Things are due to break pretty soon anyhow. Pendleton's notes will soon be due and he won't be able to meet them. But he could make it difficult for us if he knew what we are about to do." He gave them a wolfish grin. "I find myself hoping that Jones will decide to brazen it out with Schultz and that the marshal will have to shoot him for resisting arrest."

"That," approved Taylor, "would be the ideal solution."

The meeting adjourned with hearty agreement on this point.

Lance found Abner standing in the doorway of the cabin waiting for him.

"I was wonderin' whether I hadn't better buckle on my sixgun and go up there to lend you a hand," the old man said. "How'd you make out?"

Lance grinned. "Charges dismissed when I threatened to take the case to a real court. His Honor, the Mayor, and his Councilmen were present and unanimously agreed that I was a menace to the peace and security of Rossiter and ordered me out of town by noon under penalty of arrest or death at the hands of Marshal Dave Schultz, Dave to use his judgment in the matter."

"You goin'?"

"Sure. There's no reason why I should hang around town any longer."

"Rossiter and his bunch are gonna think you're scared of Schultz."

Lance shrugged. "Let them think it. I'm not afraid of them; you're never afraid of anything you scorn. I pulled a bluff and told them I was wise to them and intended to pull them down from their high places, but right now

I haven't any idea how I'm going to do it. But I'll find a way, and until I do I'm going to sit back and be the Avenger Cattle Company, L. Jefferson Jones, manager."

"That's a right fancy name."

"Mother called me Lancelot and Dad added the Jefferson in honor of President Davis."

He rigged his horse, tied his blanket roll behind the saddle, said goodbye to Abner and rode slowly along the street. As he was passing the hotel he saw Dave come from the lobby and stride towards him. Lance drew rein and looked down at him. Schultz said, "You're wise to be leavin'."

"I'm scared," said Lance. "I might keep right on to Mexico."

Schultz scowled. "Show up in Rossiter again and you'll wish you had. I'm kinda sorry you ain't puttin' up some kind of an argument about goin', but I reckon you ain't got the guts to stand up to a real man."

"I really don't know, Dave; I've never been up against one. Look around, and if you find one I might come back just to see what happens." He rode on, leaving Schultz staring after him.

He entered the trail which followed the creek and when he neared the ford where the cattle had crossed that moonlit night he heard the splash of water and knew that somebody was crossing to his side of the creek. When he came to the break in the trees two riders were just emerging and he saw that they were Colonel Pendleton and Nancy. Nancy threw him a quick glance and he instinctively touched his hat brim.

Her face froze into a mask of dislike and she said something to her grandfather. Pendleton flashed him a cold stare, then they put their horses to a lope, ignoring his salutation.

Lance grinned wryly and fished for the makings. He said to his horse, "The Princess is mad at us for the insult we tendered her when we refused to dance with her. That was her first lesson in humility; wait until we start twisting tails in earnest."

The ranch house was deserted when he reached it, the crew being busy with their roundup and tally. There were ample supplies in the house and he cooked himself a dinner and went in search of them. He located them at the upper end of the valley where they were segregating the cattle he had bought from those bearing the Stars and Bars and the Circle C, and announced his intention of working with them.

They were busy for a week, during which time Joe Stacy returned from the county seat with a wagonload of wire. They tallied their stock, then drove the Stars and Bars and Circle C stuff down the valley before them. Then the whole crew was put to work cutting fence posts.

They spent another week at this, then, satisfied that they had enough for their needs, moved down the valley to the Clark boundary and started work.

They started the fence among the trees which fringed the base of the hills, stretching the wire from trunk to trunk until they reached open range. Markers at the corners of the Clark quarter-section were used as guides.

The Clark buildings were plainly visible not more than half a mile away and they hadn't been working long before Lance saw two horsemen approaching from that direction. He had donned work clothes and was at the far end of the line digging post holes. As the riders drew near he recognized Ben Clark and judged the man with him to be Ben's father. He turned his back so that Ben would not recognize him.

The two pulled up by the wagon and Ben asked sharply, "Who's in charge here?"

Joe Stacy detached himself from the men and moved towards them. "I am."

"What are you men doing here?"

"I reckon we're fixin' to string some fence."

"Where?"

"Along this line to the marker, then around the corner to the other one, then along the Pendleton line to the other side of the valley."

"Do you realize that a fence will cut us and

the Pendletons off from our grazing land? We have an agreement with Don Esteban."

"Agreement?" It was plain from Joe's tone that he didn't like Ben Clark.

"Well, call it an understanding then."

"I don't know a thing about that; all I know is that I have orders to run a fence across the valley."

Ben said shortly, "Come on, Pop; no use arguing with this fellow. We'll hunt up Don Esteban and do our talking to him."

They cut straight across the range in the direction of the distant *hacienda*. Joe came over to where Lance stood and Lance gave him a grin. "They'll have quite a ride if they expect to find Don Esteban."

"Let 'em ride. Danged Smart Alec! If he'd been halfway decent I woulda told him that the Don don't live here no more; but no, he's gonna deal with Don Esteban himself. Wouldn't do to talk to a common cowhand."

They went on with the work and in two hours Lance saw Ben and his father returning. Once more he turned his back. He heard the horses pull up, then came Ben's angry voice. "Where's Don Esteban? He isn't at the *hacienda*."

"I coulda told you that," came Joe's drawl, "if you hadn't been so all-fired set on findin' him yourself. He's somewhere in Mexico."

"Mexico! Why didn't you tell me instead of letting us ride all the way to the *hacienda*?"

"You didn't ask me. And don't try gettin' tough, young feller. The Don sold out to the Avenger Cattle Company and left the valley a couple weeks ago."

"Sold out!" There was consternation in Ben's voice. "He never said a word to us about selling out. Who runs this Avenger Cattle Company?"

"I do business with their agent; if you got any kick comin' let me know and I'll pass it along to him."

"I'll deal with him myself. Where can I find this agent?"

"I told you you could contact him through me."

"I'll write direct. What's his name and address?"

"You'll deal with him through me or else. Now you're holdin' up the work and besides I'm gettin' tired of talkin' to you. Run along and roll your hoop."

Ben glared at him and Joe glared back and it was Ben who finally shifted his gaze. He growled, "Come along, Pop; no use wasting time with this upstart." He wheeled his horse and they rode rapidly away. Joe once more came over to where Lance stood. "He called me an upstart; what's that mean?"

"I doubt if he knows himself. He learns those words from the gang in Rossiter. Joe, you handled that just right."

"I'm glad you're satisfied; I ain't. I shoulda yanked him off his horse and taught him some manners."

"He learned his manners from the same bunch. What they all need to be taught is how to act human." He turned to gaze at the rapidly travelling horsemen; they were headed towards the Pendleton ranch buildings.

The work went rapidly on. They had driven the chuck wagon from the headquarters ranch in order to save going back and forth for dinner, but they would return to the comfort of the bunkhouse at night. It was midafternoon when their next visitors approached. They came in a body and Lance saw the erect figure of Colonel Pendleton riding in advance. Lance said to Joe, "More company. Entertain them," and went back to the wagon where he could make himself inconspicuous and still hear the conversation.

The Stars and Bars crew came up at a run and pulled in their horses close to where Joe stood awaiting them. Colonel Pendleton's black eyes were glinting and his gray goatee seemed to bristle. He said, "I understand, suh, that Don Esteban has sold his property."

"That's right. You're Colonel Pendleton, I reckon?"

"I am, suh. I had an understanding with Don Esteban permitting my cattle to graze on his range. I am sure, suh, that he would not sell without first notifying me unless the same arrangement had been made with the new owner."

"I don't know about that, Colonel. All I know is that the Avenger Cattle Company ordered me to build this fence."

"I should like to see the owner at once, suh."

"I reckon the Clarks told you I deal with their agent. It happens that I don't know where he's gettin' his mail at the present time. All I can do is deliver a message when I meet up with him again."

"Very well. When you get in touch with him tell him to communicate with me at once. In the meantime I shall expect to use the range as I have been until I hear definitely to the contrary."

"I'm tellin' you definitely to the contrary, Colonel."

"I prefer to get word directly from the owner, suh. Good day."

The Colonel wheeled his horse, trotted back to his men and with a wave of his hand summoned them to follow him.

Joe said to Lance, "He's a peppery old boy, ain't he? But different from the Clarks. He's a real gentleman; not what you call cocky, just dignified and sure of himself."

Lance nodded. "He came out here after the war; the Stars and Bars is a plantation to him where the gods provide and his word is law."

"He's an old man, and it's a sort of shame

93

that he can't live out his life the way he's been used to livin' it."

"He'll have to be taken down a few pegs along with his granddaughter," said Lance firmly. "And don't forget, Joe, that they run with the pack that I still blame for the death of my grandfather."

"I'm not forgettin'," said Joe quietly. "I'm carryin' on accordin' to orders. Let's get at that fence."

So the work went on and the fence reached the corner of the Clark land and turned and marched on to the other corner and then turned again and followed the Pendleton boundary towards the other side of the wide valley.

They were not molested. On the far side, where the range was still open, they saw the Clarks and the Pendletons busy hazing their cattle back up the valley and Joe asked Lance if he wanted the movement stopped. Lance told him not to bother; when the fence was finished they'd make another drive through a gap left for the purpose.

"I told the Colonel I'd get in touch with that agent sooner or later," Joe said. "When are you goin' to see him?"

"I'm not. He's coming to see me. Wait until the fence is finished and the Stars and Bars cattle are back on their own range."

So the days passed and they saw only occasional riders from the Stars and Bars who had evidently approached only to observe the progress of the fence. Lance took time off to drive to Junction City in the buckboard. Here he reclaimed his trunks and valises and transported them to the *hacienda*. Upon his return to the ranch he learned from Joe that the fence had been finished and that the boys were busy driving Stars and Bars and Circle C cattle to their own side of the line.

"The Colonel sent his foreman over to find out if I'd located you yet and if so to tell you he was expectin' a visit from you," reported Joe.

"Fine. You can ride over there and tell the Colonel I'm here and will be expecting him at two o'clock tomorrow afternoon."

Joe gave him a slow grin. "Think he'll come?"

"Sooner or later he'll have to if he wants to see me."

Joe rode to the Pendleton ranch the next morning and returned shortly before noon. "He'll be over," he reported, grinning wryly. "Feller, I thought for a minute that he was gonna have me tossed off the spread for presumin' to suggest that he call on you. He got on his high horse but the gal coaxed him off'n it by tellin' him the misunderstandin' could be settled easier by not makin' an enemy of the company right off the bat. She's sure some little lady, Jonesy."

Lance felt an uncomfortable stirring within

him. "I suppose so," he answered with an assumption of indifference.

He set the stage for the Colonel's appearance. The little office was spotless, the furniture carefully arranged, and Lance decked himself out in one of the outfits he had brought from the East. The crew was out on the range, only Joe remaining at the house with him. The Colonel arrived shortly after two accompanied by his hard-faced foreman. Joe met them and ushered the Colonel into the office, ignoring the foreman who started in after the Colonel, found his way blocked and sat down on the gallery.

Joe said, "Mr. Jones, this is Colonel Pendleton of the Stars and Bars."

Lance got up and at sight of him the Colonel came near to blinking. Lance did not offer his hand. He said, "Won't you sit down, Colonel?"

Pendleton said, "So this is what brought you to Rossiter, Mr. Jones." He sank slowly into a chair, his eyes still probing Lance. Lance sat down, said, "Yes, Colonel. I came here as the agent for the Avenger Cattle Company to do business with Don Esteban Guiterras. I wanted to stay in Rossiter but some people there made it rather unpleasant. What can I do for you, sir?"

The Colonel was at a disadvantage but he braced his shoulders and plunged ahead. "About this fence, Mr. Jones. Ever since coming into the valley the Stars and Bars have had an

96

understanding with Don Esteban whereby we could use his range. Surely he mentioned the matter to you?"

"I noticed the cattle on his land and mentioned the matter to him. He said there was no agreement, that he didn't need the pasture and simply allowed you to use it."

"I should like to ask for an extension of that privilege, suh."

"I'm afraid that isn't possible. We expect to increase our herd considerably and the first step was to construct a fence to keep other cattle off our range."

"But our range is inadequate, suh. Had I known of Don Esteban's intention to sell I should have put in a bid for part of the land."

"How many cattle are you grazing, Colonel?"

"About five thousand head, suh."

Lance raised his eyebrows. "Are you sure? Judging from the number we found on our range I should say there were considerably less."

"You are mistaken, suh. Our tally last fall showed over five thousand head."

"Well, I must tell you that we will have to refuse your request for free range. If you're overstocked I'd advise you to sell off your surplus cattle. The Avenger Cattle Company will take them off your hands at a reasonable price."

"I have no desire to cut down, suh. The ranch belongs to my granddaughter and I intend to hand it over to her intact when she marries or becomes of age. If you will not grant grazing privileges, perhaps you'd consider leasing some range to us?"

"Certainly. At a price, of course."

"And that price, suh?"

"Fifty dollars, a year per acre."

"That's ridiculous! We are not buying the land."

"No. Colonel, you aren't. You couldn't buy the land at any price. It's just that we're not anxious to lease."

Pendleton stood up. "It's plain," he said stiffly, "that we can reach no agreement. I'll bid you good-day, suh."

Lance followed the stiff back to the door. He said, "It might be a good idea to consider our offer of buying your surplus stock, Colonel. If you have any surplus stock."

Pendleton did not answer. He mounted his horse and rode swiftly away, the hard-faced foreman beside him. At a fork in the trail he motioned the foreman to turn off to the ranch; he continued on to Rossiter. It was close to suppertime when he reached the town and Jacob Ordman was locking the door of his office. The Colonel stepped from his horse and said brusquely, "Let's go back inside, Jacob; I must talk with you."

Ordman ushered him into the office and the

Colonel told him of his conversation with Lance. "We must have room to graze our stock, Jacob. This agent, Jones, offered to buy stock but I will not consider cutting down our herd and I wouldn't sell to him in any event."

"Did you say *Jones?*"

"Yes suh, I did. The same fellow who hung around Rossiter until he was ordered out of town."

"So that's what brought him to Rossiter," mused Ordman. He had a feeling of relief. He went on. "I'll look up the deed, Colonel, and check it for the location of the land sold. There may be some flaw in it. In the meanwhile if you really need the range, perhaps the cattle can circle the fence or break through. Quite a number of Stars and Bars steers could mingle with the company's cattle without being detected until roundup time."

The Colonel stared at him. "I should prefer handling the matter in a legal manner, Jacob. I will leave it in your hands."

Ordman went outside with him, assuring him once more that he'd look into the matter, and when the Colonel had gone he hurried to Rossiter's home. When they were alone in the parlor he said tersely, "I've just got the lowdown on that Jones fellow. We don't need to fear him; he's the agent for the company which bought out Don Esteban."

"The Don sold out?"

"Yes. To some outfit called The Avenger Cattle Company. This fellow Jones handled the deal."

And Rossiter also said, "So that's what brought him to Rossiter!"

"Right. He wasn't sent out here by a rival company or by any prospective buyers. We can go right ahead with confidence. How soon are you going to put the screws to old Pendleton?"

"He's in deep enough right now, but we want to be sure. Another loan or two would do it."

Ordman's eyes were narrowed. "It might help if he got into a shooting war with this Jones fellow. Extra men, supplies and ammunition cost money."

"It's a thought," said Rossiter. "We really ought to bring the thing to a head; our list of prospective buyers is growing larger and some of them are quite anxious to get started. Do you think you can—ah—take care of it?"

Ordman grinned a wolfish smile. "Can I? Just watch me!"

Four

Nancy knew as soon as the Colonel came in for his belated supper that he was troubled. His face was as placid as ever but there was worry in the black eyes and his greeting of "Good evening, my dear," was a grave one.

She said, "Aunt Betsy is keeping supper warm for us, but before we eat please tell me what's bothering you, Grandad."

Aunt Betsy was their colored cook and housekeeper and had come with them from Kentucky. Uncle Toby, her husband, was their butler and handyman.

The Colonel said, "It's nothing to worry about, my dear; just a misunderstanding that I'm sure will soon be cleared up."

He smiled at her but she was not satisfied. She knew about the fence but the Colonel had assured her that Don Esteban would not possibly have sold his estate without making proper arrangements for the grazing of their cattle. Now she knew that something had gone wrong.

She took him by an arm and led him to his big armchair and made him sit down. Then she perched herself on its arm and said, "Tell me all about it."

He patted her hand. Never before had she questioned; now he felt a degree of comfort in the knowledge that he could share confidences with one he loved and who loved him. Ordman and the rest were all right, but they were Yankees; there never could be other than a tolerant friendship between them.

"It seems," he said slowly, "that Don Esteban forgot to make arrangements for us. I talked to the company's manager and he tells me we must keep our cattle on our side of the fence unless we pay him a ridiculous price for grazing rights. I consulted Jacob Ordman about it and he is going to examine the deed in an effort to find a way for us. There is just the possibility that the company did not get title to all the land."

"If we lose the grazing rights will it be very bad?"

"I'm afraid so, my dear. Our land is not sufficient for all our cattle the year round. We could sell some of the stock but I don't want to do that. This Jones fellow offered to buy, but the price he would offer would probably be as outrageous as the price he asked for grazing."

And once more the question was asked, "Did you say *Jones?*"

"Yes. You've seen him. He's the fellow who

danced with that little wench from the Wildcat Saloon and then refused to dance with you."

Nancy's lips tightened. The refusal to dance had not hurt half as much as the reason he had given for refusing. An appointment with the King of Siam! That made the refusal a deliberate insult, and it was an insult that was entirely uncalled for unless—No, that couldn't be.

She leaned over and kissed her grandfather on the cheek. "We'll find a way out, don't you think we won't. We don't need all those cattle anyway; we can sell some. And not to Mr. Jones. Come dear, I'll tell Aunt Betsy to serve supper."

The Colonel, always the optimist, found his appetite; it was Nancy who merely picked at her food. When at last they had finished the meal she saw her grandfather seated in his favorite chair smoking one of his cheroots, then, with the remark that she felt like riding, she went out to the corral, had one of the men saddle her pony and set out across the range.

She followed the trail which led to the Clark place, then cut across the range to the road and followed this to the fence. There was a gate and it was fastened with a padlocked chain. A man came riding along the fence, breaking his horse into a canter when he saw her waiting. As he approached she saw that he was tall and lean and was forking a Texas saddle. He touched the brim of his hat and said, "You want through, ma'am?"

Nancy said, "If you please. I want to see your Mr. Jones."

The cowboy leaned from his saddle and unlocked the gate. He opened it without dismounting, a neat trick if you know how to do it, and touched his hat again as she rode towards the *hacienda*.

Lance was seated on the gallery talking with Joe, and when he recognized the approaching rider he got up hastily and said, "Keep her busy, will you, Joe? I'm going to get into my glad rags. These high falutin' people lose some of their aplomb when they talk with somebody who wears the same kind of clothes that they do."

"Also," drawled Joe, "makin' 'em wait takes some of the starch outa them."

When Nancy rode up to the gallery Joe got to his feet, removed his hat and asked inquiringly, "Yes, ma'am?"

"I'd like to see Mr. Jones, please."

"Why sure, ma'am. Light your saddle and come up and sit down. Mr. Jones is busy right now but I'll tell him you're here. You're Miss Nancy Pendleton, ain't you?"

She smiled at him. "Yes, I am."

"I'm Joe Stacy, foreman of the outfit."

"I'm glad to know you, Joe."

He saw her seated in the most comfortable chair, then went into the *hacienda*. When he returned he said, "Mr. Jones will join you in a few minutes. You'll excuse me, ma'am; I've got some work to do."

He touched his hat again and left, and Nancy watched as he strode across the yard to the bunkhouse. He was tall and lean and a Texan. She saw other Texans lounging about, nice looking boys and, she was sure, capable cow hands.

This man Jones, agent of the Avenger Cattle Company—she just hadn't been able to get him out of her mind. The significance of the name had struck her as soon as she had heard it, all the more forcibly because he looked so much like that other Jones she had known four years ago. But he couldn't be the same man; she had told herself that over and over. He just couldn't be. And the name of the company, he worked for—The Avenger Cattle Company. It was an odd name for a cow outfit. It had a sinister sound.

A cool voice spoke from the doorway behind her. "You wished to see me?"

Nancy got up hastily and turned to face him. If her grandfather had been able to control his features, Nancy wasn't. She actually did blink. The mysterious Mr. Jones was faultlessly attired in the very latest style; he stood relaxed and assured, regarding her; and there was no hint of recognition in the calm blue eyes.

She said, "Yes. I'm Nancy Pendleton."

He bowed gravely. "You already know my name. Please be seated, Miss Pendleton."

She sat down and he moved a chair closer to hers and dropped into it. "Is this a business call or just a neighborly visit?"

"Primarily a business call; it depends upon the outcome of the business whether or not it will become a neighborly one." He inclined his head and she went on, "I'm hoping it will be the first of a great many neighborly calls."

He did not respond to this wish. "The business?"

"Grazing land for the Stars and Bars, Mr. Jones. My grandfather came home very much discouraged. You see, we had an understanding with Don Esteban and the news that he sold out without notifying us or providing for the continuance of the arrangement was quite a shock to him."

"That situation has already been discussed by your grandfather and myself."

"Yes, he told me." She studied him gravely. "I happen to be the owner of the Stars and Bars, and my grandfather manages it for me. I'm ashamed to confess that I've never before taken even a casual interest in the ranch. I've been away to school for most of the time and a

Pendleton lady—" she smiled faintly—"is not supposed to trouble herself with business details. But it's going to be different from now on. I intend to take an active interest in things and this is my first step." She leaned forward impulsively. "Mr. Jones, we must have more grazing space. You have much more range than you need, at least for the present. Won't you be gracious enough to permit us to use part of it until we can find a permanent solution?"

He regarded her, a little frown puckering his forehead. "In the first place, Miss Pendleton, I don't believe you have as many cattle as you think. The Colonel tells me that the last tally showed five thousand head, but I've made a pretty careful survey of the range and in addition I got some idea of the number of Stars and Bars cattle when we rounded up, and I don't believe you actually have much more than half that number."

"Oh, but you must be mistaken! We've always needed Don Esteban's range. Then too, there's the Circle C stock; the Clarks will be using our pasture now that you've barred them from yours."

"There's a very simple solution to that. Just string a line of fence from the corner where ours turns and run it along the Clark boundary. Drive their cattle back on their own range and your troubles are over."

It was Nancy who frowned now. "We couldn't do that. The Clarks are our friends."

"Yes, I know. I'm afraid you're not very particular about whom you call friends, are you, Miss Pendleton?" She was about to interrupt him but for once he skipped the manners and waved his hand for silence. "You have some friends in Rossiter, a bunch of coyotes who've taken the town away from the folks who used to call it their home."

"Mr. Jones!"

Again he waved his hand to silence her. "I'm speaking the truth and in your heart you know it. These friends at times have made you forget it. But you know real quality when you see it and you know that these friends of yours are only very cheap imitations of the real thing."

"I know nothing of the sort!" she cried indignantly. "The Rossiters, the Ordmans, the Taylors—"

Again he interrupted her. He got up and leaned over her and his voice was sharp. "You *do* know the difference. They're bullies and therefore cowards. Let me recall a little scene to your mind. It happened four years ago. You invited a poor young man to a dance in Mustang. . . ."

She gasped, "Lance!" but he went on.

"He was a poor boy. Ever since he was eight years old he worked with his grandfather grubbing for gold. He knew nothing about clothes except the Levi's and cotton shirts of the workingman. He didn't know how to dance but he liked music and he thought he could learn. He was thrilled, not because a very lovely girl had asked him to be her escort but because at last he was going to meet other boys and girls, talk with them, laugh with them, become their friends. You don't know how much that dance meant to him."

He got up and started pacing the gallery and Nancy sat there staring at him. He halted before her. "His grandfather was as happy as the boy; the old man dug up some finery he had worn when he was young and dressed the boy in it. The boy, hating his curly hair, plastered it down with bear grease. He was a sight to behold, but he didn't know any better. He walked into the hotel lobby aglow with expectation. You know what happened. Or have you forgotten?

"He was met with insults and scorn and laughter. The girl who had invited him turned away as though he were some kind of a monster. The young men of her set—these Yankee friends—ganged up on him and beat and kicked him. And the so-called ladies did nothing to stop them. And then Mark Rossiter's handpicked marshal threw him in jail, kept him there overnight, and then made a further spectacle of him by parading him along the street and ordering him out of town."

"Oh, Lance!" Her voice was stricken. "I didn't—"

He cut in again. "But that's not the worst of it; that isn't what made this young man so vengeful."

He started walking again and he spoke as he walked, almost as though he didn't care whether or not she could hear him. "During his absence, caused by these friends of yours, his grandfather, excited over some gold he had found, went into the drift they were driving when it wasn't safe to enter. If Lance had been there, as he would have been but for his detention in the Mustang jail, he would not have permitted the old man to enter without first shoring up that tunnel. But he wasn't there and Hiram Jones went in and kept digging until the ground caved in on him and killed him. Yes, killed him. That's what Lance Jones returned to that morning—a caved-in tunnel with his grandfather crushed under tons of rock and earth."

He made a final gesture and sat down abruptly, and now his shoulders sagged and he buried his face in his hands.

Nancy sat staring at him and there was a full minute of silence; then she said, "I'm sorry, Lance. So terribly sorry. The very next morning I went—but it really doesn't matter what I did, does it? Everything is so plain now. You found gold and completed your education and came back. You came back to punish."

He looked up at her, his face still distorted with grief. "Yes, to punish. When I've humbled the Pendletons I'll start on the others. I don't know how, but I will. You can tell them if you like. I've already told them that I intend to humble them." He gained control of his emotion and his face once more smoothed out. He got up with a gesture of finality.

"No, Miss Pendleton, there will be no free grazing on ACC range. I haven't called it the Avenger Cattle Company for nothing. The price I set for grazing rights was fifty dollars an acre per year; you'd be foolish to accept it. But perhaps it's beyond my power to hurt you after all. Take another tally of your stock. Supervise it personally. You may find that you have enough grazing land after all."

She got up slowly, her violet eyes fixed on him. She did not offer her hand; she was the proud Pendleton again. "I understand, Mr. Jones. I can't call you Lance; you wouldn't want me to. I was not influenced by my friends that night of the dance. I was a young girl of sixteen, and I'd bragged about you and I was terribly humiliated. I'm glad you've told me about your grandfather, for now I know the reason for the stand you've taken."

She paused and for a brief space they stood

regarding each other; then she went on. "I am awfully sorry about the accident to your grandfather, and if you are sure that your presence would have prevented it I wouldn't blame you at all for seeking revenge. But I'm afraid I can see it only as an unfortunate coincidence. Perhaps without your being conscious of it the real source of your desire for vengeance comes from hurt pride, from the humiliation you suffered on that miserable night. But thank you for explaining. Good evening, Mr. Jones."

She walked proudly down the steps and swung into her saddle. He did not accompany her, but stood watching as the dusk swallowed her. Then he sighed and once more his shoulders sagged. The victory was his but somehow he could not relish it.

Nancy rode rapidly, but the darkness was deep when at last she came to the gate. The lanky Texan let her through and she thanked him absently. Her mind was seething. It had been Lance after all, a more mature Lance, a Lance who had become a man of the world, a person of wealth and consequence. And he had come back to punish. They could expect no consideration from him.

She shook her curls with a quick despairing movement of her head. He might *think* he was avenging the death of his grandfather; at the time of the accident she had no doubt that he believed them the cause of the tragedy. But that was four years ago; surely in the intervening time he must have seen the flaw in this line of reasoning. The cave-in might have occurred even if they had shored up the walls, or Hiram's excitement might have communicated itself to Lance and he might have gone in with his grandfather and met the same fate. His attitude was wrong, all wrong; but still—she thought of her own grandfather; suppose he had been the victim, how would she feel?

As for their Yankee friends, she did know the difference between them and the people she had associated with in Louisville; she accepted them because they maintained a semblance of social life as she had become used to it. Lance had been right there, but she could not admit it because these people had always been kind and considerate. Just look how they had welcomed her home! The town decorated, a lovely dinner with complimentary speeches, a big dance. Such a gala affair had cost lots of money and Mark Rossiter and the others had footed the bill. Or had they? Sudden doubt brought consternation to her face, but she swept it aside after a moment. Of course they had. But suddenly the matter became very important to her.

It was fairly late when she finally rode into the yard and she noticed that the bunkhouse was dark. She frowned; she hadn't thought it *that* late; some of the crew usually remained up until midnight playing cards. There was a light in the house and her grandfather called from the gallery, "Nancy? Where have you been, child?"

"Just riding, Grandad," she called back. "Be with you in a minute."

A figure shuffled out of the darkness and the voice of old Uncle Toby said, "Ah'll put up yo' hors, Miz Nancy. Sho' looks lak everybody in the crew's done turned in. You run up there to the Cunnel; he's been right anxious about yo'."

Nancy thanked the old servant and went up on the gallery. Her grandfather said, "You shouldn't stay out after dark, child, when you're alone."

"Nonsense, Grandad; I'm not a little girl any longer." She sat on the arm of his chair and put an arm about his shoulder. "You worry too much. From now on I'm going to take some of the load off your shoulders. It's time that I did, don't you think?"

"I don't want you to worry, my dear."

She kissed him lightly on the top of his head. "I know you don't, darling; but everybody has to worry sooner or later. It's part of life. And usually the worries turn out to be needless and after you've shaken them off you feel so much lighter and gayer. I think I've been missing something." And because she did want to relieve him of worry she did not tell him that the agent of The Avenger Cattle Company, its owner, in fact, was the boy they had humiliated four years before. She realized suddenly that she couldn't tell anybody this because if she did word of it would get to this old man whom she loved so dearly.

There was something uppermost in her mind and she had to dispose of it. She said, "I was thinking tonight that I've thanked everybody but you for the wonderful reception they gave me when I came home. It was very thoughtless, for you really arranged everything, didn't you?" She knew it was a bit late to bring this matter up but she could think of no other way of getting the information she wanted.

The Colonel said, "It was very little, my dear."

"It was not at all little. The decorations, the lovely dinner, the dance—you paid for it, didn't you, darling?"

"Of course. Mr. Rossiter suggested that we have some sort of welcoming home party. It was stupid of me not to think of it myself."

"It wasn't at all; you've been so very wonderful to me." She gave him a little hug and they sat in silence for a moment. Then she asked, "Just how many cattle are we grazing, Grandad?"

"Our last tally showed a few over five thousand head."

"That many?"

"Yes. That man Jones—" she felt him stiffen— "had the effrontery to doubt my word."

"He's an idiot. You couldn't be mistaken, you probably tallied them yourself."

"Certainly not, my dear. We have a competent crew to work our cattle."

"The crew," said Nancy musingly. She was doing very well at getting the information she wanted. "When Daddy was living I knew them all, but now they're all strangers to me. I've been away so much and I suppose they keep dropping off."

"Yes. I'm afraid your father spoiled them; they never seemed contented after we lost him. Jacob Ordman suggested some changes; we hired a foreman of his selection, Buck Borden, and he began tightening up on them. The old hands gradually dropped out and were replaced. Our present crew is very efficient. Hard working boys, all of them."

"And you trust Mr. Ordman's judgment, of course."

"Naturally, child. He's a Yankee—all of them are—but they've been very kind. And most Yankees are shrewd business men."

She knew by the inflection of his voice that he sensed the difference, too. She got up. "It's past your bedtime, and I'm sorry I kept you up. I won't do it again."

They went into the house together and he kissed her and retired. Uncle Toby came in and proceeded to lock up. Nancy wished him goodnight and went to her room. She undressed and got into bed but she didn't sleep for a long time. Thoughts were milling about in her head, disturbing thoughts. The reception for which she had given their Yankee friends credit they didn't deserve; Lance's implication that their cattle numbered less than the tally sheets had shown; the complete change in the crew; her grandfather's reliance on the lawyer, Ordman.

Loyalty fought a stubborn battle; Ordman and the rest had been so good, there was no proof that they were other than they pretended. Perhaps they were a bit conceited, a trifle arrogant, but in their crude surroundings they could not be blamed so much for feeling a bit above their neighbors. Or could they?

She remembered that before their coming she had played with Mexican and Indian kids and was something like a younger sister to the cowboys on the spread. If one of them had appeared at a dance in his working clothes she would not have snubbed him. Was it possible that Lance was right and that she had been influenced by these Rossiter friends of theirs?

She fell into a troubled sleep at last, and how long she slept she did not know. She awakened with a start and the distinct impression that it had been the sound of a distant shot which had awakened her. She sat up in bed, straining her ears. The sound was not repeated and slowly she came to the conclusion that it had been the wind slamming a shutter. She wasn't entirely convinced that this was the case, but the silence persisted and finally she lay down again.

She found it impossible to go back to sleep. She tossed about and changed positions a dozen time and finally got up, slipped into a robe and sat by the open window. The range was wrapped in soft, shimmering moonlight and the breeze was cool and soft. She sat there for over an hour and found herself blinking. Soothed and relaxed, she went back to bed and slept soundly.

Lance had difficulty in sleeping too. He sat on the gallery and smoked long after the boys in the bunkhouse had retired. The moon came up and he too gazed out over the range. He was thinking of Nancy and the thoughts were disturbing.

She had been genuinely sorry, he knew that. He had read the distress in her eyes when he told of his grandfather's death. He heard her stricken cry, "Oh, Lance, I didn't—" Didn't what? Understand? Mean to hurt you? Why hadn't he let her finish.

And then, "I'm sorry, Lance. So terribly sorry. The next morning I went—well, it really doesn't matter what I did, does it?" Why hadn't she told him what she'd done? If, for instance, she had said that she tried to find him, to apologize, to make amends, it would have made all the difference in the world. But she hadn't told him. She hadn't offered any defense whatever except that she had been only sixteen and had been deeply humiliated.

And finally she had told him that perhaps it was just hurt pride which motivated him in his scheme of vengeance. Not consciously, of course, but using the death of Hiram Jones as a cloak for the real motive, fortifying himself with the belief that they were responsible.

He shifted uncomfortably in the chair and flung his cigarette from him. Hell, he was getting soft. Anybody could see through it. Grandfather had failed to get the concession of free range and so the lovely Nancy had tried her hand, hoping to win through by her charm and a man's instinctive reluctance to hurt a woman.

He heard sounds at the holding corral and realized that a night rider was going out to take the fence shift from midnight to dawn. Time he was going to bed. He got up and paced about the gallery. He heard the man ride off into the moonlight and went to his room. He undressed and lay for a long while on the bed smoking. Nancy. Why couldn't he stop thinking of her?

He heard the relieved rider come in and knew

it was after one. He crushed out his cigarette and pulled the covers over him. He forced himself to relax and finally fell into a light sleep.

He too awoke with the impression that it was a shot which had awakened him and he too sat up in bed, listening. There was no other sound. He got up and went to a window and looked out. The moon was waning. He stayed there for a long while and heard nothing more. He went back to bed and slept.

At dawn he awakened feeling tired and dispirited. He got up, doused his face with cold water and towelled briskly. He felt no better. He built a fire in the kitchen stove and put sliced bacon in the pan to sizzle and coffee to boil. He heard his Texans calling to one another, joking and laughing. He ate slowly but without relish.

A pall of despondency hung over him and he was angry at himself for letting this girl get under his skin. Had she been right? Was it just hurt pride that was driving him? He didn't give a hoot about the Rossiter crowd; he owed them plenty for what they had done to him and he intended to see to it that they got what was coming to them. But the Pendletons; they were Southerners like himself. And after all she had been but sixteen.

Why not call the whole thing off as far as they were concerned? He didn't need all that range. Tear down the fence and say, "Come on in, neighbor, and help yourself." He could see the gratitude shining in her violet eyes, he could hear her soft whisper, "Oh, Lance! Thank you so much."

He felt better. He tackled the remaining bacon and fried two more eggs. He ate with gusto and washed down the food with another cup of coffee. He washed the dishes and whistled while he did it. He'd tell Joe to tear down the fence and he'd ride over to the Pendletons himself with the good news.

He strode through the doorway and halted on the gallery. Coming towards the house at a hard run was a horseman and in the early light he recognized one of his Texans. The speed at which he was coming spelled trouble of some kind.

Lance went down the steps and rounded the corner of the house. The men were at the corral saddling up but they had ceased operations to stare at the approaching rider. Lance called sharply, "Joe!" and Stacy walked over to join him. Lance asked, "I wonder what happened to bring him in?"

"I sure don't know. He ain't just takin' his mornin' exercise and it ain't Slim Hawkins hittin' the high spots on his way to breakfast. That's Bud Kelly, the boy who rode out to relieve Slim at dawn."

Bud Kelly came sweeping into the yard on a sweating horse. He was grimfaced and his eyes were narrowed. He checked his horse with a quick jerk on the rein and said abruptly, "Slim's dead. Layin' out there near where the gate was. There ain't no more gate; there ain't no more fence. They ripped it up, burned the posts and tangled the wire so it cain't be used for nothin' again."

The news held them silent and for a moment there was a tableau of rigid forms and grim, staring faces; then as though galvanized by the same current men went on with their saddling. But they worked rapidly now and there was no exchange of banter. Lance caught up his horse and cinched on the saddle. They cut swiftly across the range and before they reached the boundary line they saw the piles of smoking posts which extended across the valley.

Slim Hawkins lay where he had fallen, on his back, his arms outflung, unseeing eyes turned towards the heavens. The men dismounted and stood looking down at the lifeless body. Slim had been shot through the heart and the clothing about the wound was singed. He had been shot at pointblank range.

Lance got a blanket from his saddle roll, spread it over Slim and weighed the corners down with stones. They remounted, still in grim silence. There was no need of an order; they headed automatically for the Pendleton ranch house.

It was midmorning when they entered its yard and the Texans rode straight to the bunkhouse. Lance and Joe swerved and made for the house and as they approached it both Colonel Pendleton and Nancy came out. They halted at the gallery and swung to the ground; they uttered no word of greeting as they ascended the low steps. Pendleton demanded sternly, "What is the meaning of this intrusion? What right have your crew to make themselves at home in our bunkhouse without invitation?"

"They're looking for the men who destroyed our fence and shot one of our men."

The Colonel stared. Nancy uttered a stifled gasp. "Oh, no!"

Lance said grimly, "Don't try to tell me you know nothing about it."

"But we don't! I tell you we don't!"

"How do you know that it was done by our crew?" asked the Colonel.

"Who else would have done it? Not the Clarks; the fence ran clear across the valley and the two of them couldn't have done all the damage in the time they had. It was your men; where are they?"

Pendleton made a vague gesture. "Out on the range, suh, attending to their duties, I suppose."

123

"Just where?"

"I don't know. My foreman attends to all range work."

"You're not a very efficient manager, Colonel. But you must have given the order to tear down our fence. They wouldn't do that on their own."

"I gave no such order, suh. The crew retired early last night. I sat here on the gallery waiting for Nancy and they were in their bunks at ten o'clock."

"And got out again at twelve."

Nancy said, "I'm sure they didn't. We went right to bed but I didn't sleep very well and I would have heard them at the corral."

Lance studied her broodingly. In his heart he did not believe that she had any knowledge of what had happened. He was inclined to believe the same thing of the Colonel but he could not be sure.

The Texans came riding around the corner of the house and one of them reported, "Not a sign of them anywhere, but they haven't hit the trail because they's bedrolls and rifles in the bunkhouse."

"We'll find them," said Lance, and went down the steps with Joe. They swung into their saddles and the whole body of horsemen spurred out of the yard. Joe looked over his shoulder and ran his eyes over the men behind them. He asked, "Where's Bud Kelly?"

One of them answered. "Reckon he's still lookin' around. Him and Slim were buddies."

They spent the rest of the day scouring the Stars and Bars range in a search for the crew. They did not find Buck Borden and his men and finally Lance led his party homeward. They halted at the place where Slim lay and made a litter of poles which could be fastened to a horse like a pair of shafts. They spread a blanket over this and lashed Slim's body fast and transported it to the ranch in that manner. There they dug a grave on a grassy knoll and buried him, and the darkness was thick when at last they had their supper. But Kelly had not returned.

When they had eaten they saddled up again and Lance called the men about him He said, "I know how you boys feel about Slim's death, but I don't want any of you flying off the handle. We want to be sure where the blame rests before we start anything."

One of them said grimly, "Reckon we'll take our orders from Joe, Mr. Jones. You're just the agent of the company."

"I *am* the company," Lance told them quietly. "I bought this land as part of a scheme to pay the Pendletons and their Rossiter friends a debt of long standing. The fence was part of that scheme and Slim's death comes right home to me. The man who shot him will hang, I promise you that; but we're not going to hang the wrong man and so you fellows are going to let me run the show."

There was a moment of surprised silence, then the man said, "That puts a different light on it. We'll do as you say, Mr. Jones; but if we get our hands on Slim's killer, don't ask us to show him no mercy."

"If we get our hands on him, I'll help pull the rope. And from here on the Mr. Jones is out. I'm Lance. Let's ride."

They headed once more for the Stars and Bars pulling down to a walk when they were still some distance away. The moon had not yet risen and it was dark. They saw a light in the house but the crew's quarters were dark. Lance led them to a clump of trees at the base of the hills and they dismounted there and tied their horses. A man was sent to reconnoiter and he returned to report that both corral and bunkhouse were empty. The Stars and Bars men had not yet returned to get their personal belongings.

They waited at the edge of the trees in grim silence. The light in the ranch house blinked out and the moon came up. Lance, becoming restless, said to Joe in a low voice, "What do you think, Joe? Is my hunch wrong?"

"I don't think so, Lance. I figger they'll wait until daylight when they can look down from the hills and see the whole valley. If they don't spot us they'll figger the way's clear for them."

The night dragged by, the moon waned and the gray of dawn showed in the sky. Another hour passed and the sun came up. They waited patiently. And then they heard the soft cracking of brush off to their left and the unmistakable thud of hoofs. A file of men rode from the trees and loped their horses across the open space and dismounted outside the bunkhouse. They left their mounts ground-anchored and went into the building. Lance said, "All right, boys. We won't need the horses."

He started at a run towards the bunkhouse, Joe beside him and the rest of them close on their heels. They were fifty yards from the building when a man came out. He was carrying a blanket roll and a rifle and at sight of them he stopped abruptly, mouth open, sudden fear in his eyes; then he leaped inside and slammed the door. As they came up at a run they heard the grate of a bar as it was dropped into place.

Lance thumped on the door. "You might as well come out with your hands in the air. And make it fast."

They heard confused sounds, the voices of men in dispute, then came the answer, "If you want us you'll have to come in and get us."

Lance stepped back to survey the building. It was solidly built of logs and adobe and he doubted that the door could be easily forced. Unless they were content to camp here until the occupants were starved out, the capture of the Stars and Bars men would mean the lives of some of his Texans. He didn't want that; this was his feud.

And then while he considered they heard another voice. It came from within the cabin and it was harsh and rasping. It said, "Git yore paws in the air, you sons of pups! Git 'em up!"

Joe swore. "That's Bud Kelly. He's been hidin' there since yeste'day layin' for 'em."

Bud spoke again. "That's right. Keep 'em up. You in the front, unbar that door."

They heard the rasp of the bar as it was removed and Lance pushed the door open. His Colt was levelled and his men were close behind him when he stepped into the room.

Buck Borden and his men were scattered about the room, some seated on bunks, some kneeling on the floor making up bed rolls, a few standing. Bud was crouched behind a bunk at the far end of the long room holding them under his gun and his face was a cold, hard mask.

Bud said, "You fellers would have to horn in on my play. If you'd let me handle it I'd have found Slim's killer in a hurry or blasted every one of these lousy coyotes!"

"We'll find him," promised Lance. "Joe, collect their guns."

Joe disarmed them and Lance asked, "Who's foreman of this outfit?"

"I am," said Buck Borden.

Lance surveyed him intently. He was the man who had ordered him off the Stars and Bars range that day when Dave Schultz had tried and failed. Lance said, "I remember you. You'd better talk mighty fast and straight. Which one of you shot my fence guard?"

"None of us shot him," answered Borden.

"That's a danged lie!" cried Bud Kelly hotly.

"It ain't no lie," said another of the crew. "None of us shot him."

"Tell us you didn't tear down our fence and maybe we'll believe that, too," snapped Lance.

"Yeah, we tore down the fence," growled Borden, "but none of us shot the guard. That's straight."

A voice spoke from the doorway. "Who ordered you to tear down the fence?"

Lance turned his head and saw Nancy Pendleton standing in the doorway. She stood erect, her hands clenched into fists at her sides. Behind her was the Colonel, white of face and looking old and tired. Nancy's gaze was on Buck Borden, and she repeated, *"Who ordered you to tear down the fence?"*

Borden's gaze shifted. "That was our own idea."

"That's another lie," said Lance flatly, "but we won't go into it now. What we want to know is who killed Slim Hawkins. You tore down

129

the fence so one of you must have done it. I'm going to find out who it was if I have to turn every one of you over to Bud Kelly and let him work you over."

Borden glared at him defiantly, but the other men glanced uneasily at the glowering Kelly and then at each other. Nobody spoke. Lance said impatiently, "Joe, fetch the horses. We'll take this bunch to the ranch and see if we can loosen their tongues."

Joe went out. Nancy and the Colonel came into the bunkhouse and Nancy came forward to where Lance stood. She said, "What are you going to do with them?"

"Ask Bud Kelly; it's his party."

She asked tightly, "Torture?"

"Yes. Somebody stood right in front of Slim talking to him and shot him through the heart before he knew what to expect. Anybody who'd cover up for a filthy murderer like that deserves to be tortured."

"I—Oh, it's horrible! Horrible! But Grandfather and I had nothing to do with it. Please believe me when I say that."

"Not the killing. I don't know about the fence. Somebody gave them their orders; who else could it be?"

She moved past him and walked up to one of the Stars and Bars men. She stood in front of him and held his gaze with her eyes. She said,

"Bill, you're about the only one on the crew I really know. I want you to tell me the truth. Who ordered you to tear down the fence? I don't care who's hurt, I want to know."

The man shifted his gaze, but she put her hands on his arms and said, "No, don't turn your head. Look at me. I want to know. Who told you to do it?"

He kept his tortured gaze on her for another moment, then jerked loose and made a violent gesture with his arms. "Aw, hell, what's the use, fellers? Why should we cover up for a killer because of a few lousy bucks?" His eyes came around to her again and his face was tight. He blurted, "It was Ben Clark. He hired us to tear down the fence and he shot the man himself."

Borden cursed. "Damn you, Bill! I'll bust you—"

Bud Kelly leaped forward and struck him on the mouth. Bud's eyes were burning. "Shut your yap! You'll bust nobody. Go ahead, feller, talk!"

"That's it," said Bill. "Ben done business with Buck Borden. We were to get ten dollars apiece for pullin' down the fence. The killin' wasn't in it. We moved our horses from the corral to the trees soon's it was dark and turned in early. At midnight we snuck out and rode to the fence. Ben joined us and rode ahead to scout. We was half a mile away when it happened and we rode up to find out what the shootin' was about.

"Ben was standin' over the dead guard. We didn't know what to do. We stood around waitin' but nothin' happened and finally Ben said to get busy on the fence and he'd see that we got fifty apiece instead of ten. He said we'd plant the feller and nobody'd know what happened to him, but when we got through with the fence and was fixin' to bury him we heard his relief man comin' and got out of there fast. That's the straight of it."

"It's enough for me," said Bud Kelly. "Me, I'm callin' on Ben Clark."

He wheeled and stalked through the doorway and the others crowded out after him. Lance halted before Pendleton. The Colonel had sagged against the door frame and he was a beaten old man. Lance said, "The death of Slim Hawkins is pinned on Ben Clark, but your men tore down the fence and you're responsible for their actions. That fence must be rebuilt by your crew and I must be paid compensation."

The Colonel straightened with an effort. "The fence will be rebuilt, suh. You have my word for it."

"And the compensation?"

"You will be compensated."

"In the amount of five thousand dollars."

The Colonel did not blink an eye. He was the proud Pendleton once more.

"You shall have that amount as soon as I can get it from the bank, suh."

Lance strode from the room and swung into his saddle. The men were already thundering towards the Circle C. He rode fast to overtake them, but presently he turned to look back.

The Colonel and Nancy were standing outside the bunkhouse looking after them. They stood erect and proud and their arms were about each other.

Lance swore bitterly. He had defeated them but they refused to be humbled. And they had not been guilty either of the destruction of the fence or the death of Slim Hawkins. Perhaps he had misjudged them; perhaps they themselves were the victims of the scheming men who dominated Rossiter.

Ben Clark. He was aware of a sudden thrill as he realized that this would be the end of Ben's dream to possess the Stars and Bars. Ben had given the order to tear down the fence, Ben had shot Slim. Was he acting on his own, or had he in turn received the order from someone higher up?

The thought intrigued him. Ben had nothing to gain by removing the fence because he still had grazing land which belonged to his friends, the Pendletons. The whole thing began to smell. And the odor was definitely Rossiter!

Five

It was close to noon when Lance and his Texans rode into the yard of the Circle C. Except for a single horse in the corral the place had the appearance of utter desolation. Several of the Texans rode around to the rear of the house; the others sat their saddles, alert and watchful, as Lance and Joe swung to the ground and mounted the gallery steps.

The front door was open and they entered. They heard the scrape of a chair in the kitchen and strode towards the doorway to be met there by the elder Clark. He was wiping his ragged moustache on his sleeve and had evidently been eating dinner.

Lance asked sharply, "Where's Ben?"

"He ain't here. Whadda you want with him?"

"He murdered one of my men. If we find him we're going to hang him."

Clark stared stupidly. "He ain't here," he repeated.

"We'll make sure of that."

They searched the house thoroughly but did not find Ben Clark. The old man moved about the house with them, his face inscrutable. When they had finished he asked, "Who'd Ben kill and when?"

Lance told him curtly. Clark said, "I heerd 'em workin' on the fence and I reckon I heerd a shot. Ben didn't come home."

Lance didn't waste breath asking where Ben might be; the old man wouldn't tell them even if he knew. They went outside and were told that the crew's search of the grounds had been equally barren of result. They rode back past the Stars and Bars, following the creek road into Rossiter. They drew up before Marshal Schultz's office and Lance flung himself from his horse and strode through the doorway. Schultz was on his feet behind his desk and at sight of Lance his mouth flew open and he gasped, "You!"

"That's right. Where's Ben Clark?"

Dave closed his mouth and shook his head. "I dunno." He had told Lance what to expect if he returned to Rossiter, but the sight of the grim-faced Texans outside discouraged any summary action at this time. He said, "Whadda you want with him?"

"He murdered a man in cold blood. It's your job to arrest him if he shows in town. We're going to see if he's here and I wouldn't advise you to interfere."

Dave took another look at the Texans and said, "Go right ahead. If Ben's a killer I ain't standin' in the way of his apprehension."

Lance turned his back on the man and went outside. He saw Abner Stacy standing by Joe's horse talking with his son. Joe said, "Pops says he hasn't seen Ben around town for two days."

Lance exchanged greetings with the old man. "He may be hiding out with his friends. We'll search the town."

They did a good job of it, going through every building in Rossiter including the homes of the mighty in spite of their indignant protests. They didn't find Ben Clark and finally trooped into the Taylor House and demanded supper.

They discussed the matter while they ate. Ben Clark had probably taken to the hills and to hunt him down would be next to impossible. They decided that their best bet was to keep a close watch on the Pendleton and Circle C ranch houses and to have a man stationed close to town where Abner could contact him quickly in case Ben showed up.

They had to leave it there. For the moment Ben Clark was safe.

Nancy and her grandfather stood outside the bunkhouse looking after Lance and his Texans until a ridge hid them from view; then the Colonel stiffened and withdrew his arm from about her. "I'm going to discharge Buck Borden and his men. I'm going to send them packing now."

He turned towards the bunkhouse but she grasped him by an arm and halted him. "You promised you'd rebuild the fence, Grandfather; why not make them do it? They tore it down."

His dark eyes brightened in approval. "You're right, my dear."

They re-entered the bunkhouse and the Colonel said shortly, "You heard me promise Mr. Jones that we'd rebuild the fence. Borden, see that the men are supplied with tools, take them into the hills and set them to cutting posts."

Borden scowled, undecided; then realized that the cutting would be under his supervision and they could do some soldiering back there in the hills. He said, "Okay, Colonel. You heard the order, boys. Unstrap them saddle rolls and get tools out of the shed. Peeler, hitch up a wagon; we'll need it to haul the posts."

The Colonel and Nancy went over to the house and the Colonel buckled on the cartridge belt and pistol he had worn in the war and Nancy donned a pair of Levi's and a woolen shirt that had belonged to her father. She piled her curls on the top of her head and drew a Stetson over them, then strapped on her pearl-handled thirty-eight. They went to the corral together and she caught up their horses and saddled them. When Buck and his crew rode out of the yard they rode behind them.

There was no soldiering, and when they came

in for dinner a scowling Buck Borden came to the house and demanded his time. The Colonel said sternly, "None of the men will be paid until that fence is finished. You tore it down and you'll replace it. If you quit, the wages due you will be withheld."

So Buck, sullen and scowling, went back to work. From then on all work was done under the watchful eye of the Colonel or Nancy or both of them.

The next morning the Colonel rode to Rossiter and told his troubles to Jacob Ordman. A bit to his surprise, Ordman did not rebuke him for agreeing to pay indemnity for the destruction of the fence. He had the Colonel sign another mortgage note, went down to the bank himself and returned with the five thousand dollars.

That evening the Colonel and Nancy rode over to the old Guiterras *hacienda* to find Lance and Joe smoking on the gallery. They lingered only long enough to deliver the money and get a receipt for it. The receipt was signed The Avenger Cattle Company, L. Jefferson Jones, Agent. Nancy, Lance felt sure, had not informed her grandfather who L. Jefferson Jones really was, and for some strange reason was reluctant to do so himself.

The days passed and became weeks and the weeks a month. The fence was rebuilt and the Stars and Bars crew rounded up and drove to their side of the line all the Pendleton cattle on Avenger range. And then at Nancy's insistence a new count of their stock was taken.

The result of that count dismayed them. Instead of five thousand head they had something over twenty-five hundred, and they knew the count was correct because they had supervised it themselves. They counted them a second time and got the same result. It left them stunned.

They discussed it worriedly while they picked at their food. If the former tally had been correct, some twenty-five hundred head of cattle had disappeared into nothingness in less than a year. But had the former count been correct?

Nancy asked, "How long have you had the present crew, Grandfather?"

"Three years."

"Then if Buck Borden and his crew are dishonest they may have been stealing from us the whole time and covering up with a false tally."

The Colonel got up and squared his shoulders. "We'll fetch Buck Borden in and have it out with him," he said.

He strode out of the room, his fists clenched in anger. There was a light in the bunkhouse and the door stood open; he stepped across the sill and came to an abrupt halt. The place was empty and bedrolls and rifles and duffle bags were gone. He walked quickly to the corral. It was dark, but there was enough starlight to show him that there were just two horses in the enclosure. They would be his and Nancy's. The Colonel sagged against a corral post and bitterness welled up within him.

The finishing blow came the next day. Jacob Ordman came driving out from town with a message from the bank. Mr. Rossiter wanted to see the Colonel at once. It was very urgent and he would appreciate it if the Colonel would call at the bank before two that afternoon. He was a different Jacob Ordman than the one they had known; he was stiff and formal and left immediately after delivering the message.

"What in the world does Mr. Rossiter want in such a hurry?" wondered Nancy. "Grandfather, have you been borrowing from the bank?"

"Occasionally, my dear. A few loans, amply secured, of course."

"Yes," she said absently, "they would have to be. I'm going with you."

He tried to dissuade her, but she was insistent and he was too dispirited to argue the matter.

They drove to town immediately after dinner and were shown into Mark Rossiter's office. Jacob Ordman was there, looking solemn. Rossiter, in contrast to his usual genial heartiness, greeted them coldly. He waved them into chairs and seated himself behind his desk. He said, "Colonel, I understand that you actually have just about half the number of cattle you stated you owned when you gave us a chattel mortgage on them."

Pendleton said, "It seems, suh, that a dreadful mistake has been made somewhere. Our last tally showed five thousand head, but we just finished counting and there are only a little over twenty-five hundred."

"I hold a number of demand notes of yours, given over a period of the last three years and secured by chattel mortgage on five thousand head of stock. Since you have only half that number you are technically guilty of obtaining money under false pretenses."

"There was no false pretense, suh," said the Colonel stiffly. "I was unaware that our stock had dwindled; I believed we had five thousand head."

"In any event, the security has shrunk to such an alarming extent that the bank must protect itself by demanding payment of these notes at once."

The Colonel made a despairing gesture and Nancy asked in a firm voice, "How much do the notes amount to, Mr. Rossiter?"

"Something like forty thousand dollars."

It was a staggering blow but she took it in stride. "Surely the cattle and the land and buildings are sufficient to cover that amount."

"We hold no mortgage on the land or buildings.

They would be no good to us at all. Of the cattle, only a small percentage will fetch top price, and at a forced sale—I tell you we simply can't take further chances. The sale of the cattle will liquidate the debt and leave something over for you."

"But to sell our cattle! Mr. Rossiter, you just can't do that!"

He gave her a thin smile. "How otherwise can you meet these notes?"

The Colonel bowed his head. "I've been a fool," he groaned. "I didn't realize it was so much." He raised his head and fixed his gaze on Ordman. "I depended upon you, suh, for guidance. You let me borrow and spend without protest. You must have seen how things were going."

Ordman shook his head sadly. "I was under the impression, Horatio, that you were the owner of five thousand head of stock."

Pendleton turned his stricken gaze on Rossiter. "You mean to sell us out, to take our cattle. I counted you my friend, Mark; I never dreamed you'd do that to me."

"I'm sorry, Horatio, but this is business. Asking me to take a possible loss of forty thousand dollars is stretching friendship too far."

"Yes," said Nancy quietly, "I'm sure it is." She was thinking of Lance and her heated defense of her "friends."

Ordman cleared his throat. "Look here, Mark. I know you don't want to put Horatio out of business completely. Why not compromise? Take, say, only a thousand head of cattle and have the Colonel deed you a strip of his land for the balance." He looked hopefully at Rossiter. The scene had been carefully rehearsed.

Rossiter said, "We have no use for the land, Jacob. You know that."

"I'm not so sure, Mark. A strip at this end of the valley adjoining the town, say a mile wide and extending across the six miles of valley, might be worth something someday. Rossiter is bound to expand, and it would do for factories, or farms, or possibly a new residential area. I think it would be a good gamble. And it would help our friends. With a reduced number of cattle they wouldn't miss the range, and they would be able to remain in business."

Rossiter was gazing across the room, a frown of concentration on his face. There was a short silence, then he said, "You may be right, Jacob. Rossiter is bound to grow. And, as you say, we have no desire to put our friends out of business. How would such a settlement suit you, Horatio?"

The Colonel shook his head. "I've nothing more to say, suh. I can no longer trust my judgment. You must ask my granddaughter."

"How about it, Nancy?" urged Ordman. "The bank will sell off a thousand head of cattle, leaving you fifteen hundred. Quite a nice herd. A strip of range a mile wide and six miles across would never be missed. In return, all these notes marked paid, principal and interest. A clean start."

There was a lump of lead in Nancy's stomach. From five thousand head of cattle they would be reduced to fifteen hundred; six square miles of fertile land would be lost to them. But there was no alternative. She said, "It's a deal, Mr. Rossiter." She saw her grandfather wince and added, "We don't need or want such a large spread. The management is such a burden to Grandfather. I've never before realized how much of a burden it must have been. I'm sure we'll be very happy on a smaller ranch, won't we, Grandfather?"

She smiled at him and his eyes warmed with gratitude. "If you're satisfied, my dear, I'm sure we'll be very happy indeed."

So it was arranged, and when goodbyes had been said and the Pendletons had gone, Rossiter and Ordman exchanged significant glances. Rossiter rubbed his hands. "Very skillfully handled, Jacob; very skillfully indeed. I'll get in touch with the surveyors at once and the Rossiter Development Company can now come out into the open."

Lance had watched from a distance while the Stars and Bars cattle were being tallied and knew by the size of the herd that his guess at their number was not far off. He couldn't see, of course, the consternation which the tally brought to Nancy and the Colonel and he had no knowledge whatever of the disaster which was about to overtake them. His thought at the moment was that Colonel Pendleton was either a very inefficient manager or a very magnificent liar; he had to be one or the other to claim the possession of five thousand head of stock when the actual number was only half that.

He was sure now that the cattle he had seen being driven across the creek that moonlit night were being rustled. In all probability other cattle had been stolen, but that the herd had been reduced by half within a period of less than a year was unbelievable unless there was a lack of supervision which amounted almost to criminal negligence.

How had the thieves disposed of the stuff? The Stars and Bars brand could not be changed to anything less than a regular star-spangled banner. It was none of his business but nevertheless it bothered him. He didn't like to see the aged and the innocent swindled quite so brazenly.

When, a couple days later, one of his riders brought the information that cowboys were busy cutting out Stars and Bars cattle, Lance took a trick at the fence himself in order to see what was going on. He saw a slight figure in Levi's and wool shirt watching the work dejectedly and was able finally to convince himself that it was Nancy. He was seeing her in an entirely different light. Somehow he had never pictured her in anything but ruffled dresses and flowered bonnets.

He rode out the next day in time to see the job finished. The animals were shaped into a long column and driven past Nancy, who counted them as they moved by. The herd stretched in a long line clear to Rossiter and Lance guessed that there were a thousand steers in that column. The Pendletons were certainly selling stock and since their herd had already been so greatly diminished he wondered at it. The Colonel, he concluded, must really be up against it for cash.

Abner Stacy visited the ranch the next day and brought them the straight of it. He was bursting with excitement and indignation. "Know what?" he exploded as he dropped from his saddle and came hurrying up the gallery steps to where Lance and Joe were sitting. "That skunk of a Mark Rossiter done sold out the Pendletons. Yessir, it's a fact. Everybody in Mustang's talkin' about it. Seems that the Colonel's been borrying a hell of a lot of money for three years or more, usin' for security the five thousand head of stock he thought was wearin' the Stars and Bars. They took a tally and found they only had twenty-five hundred head and a little birdie told Mark Rossiter about it and he called the loans."

Lance gave him a cynical grin. "I thought Rossiter was such a good friend."

"Feller, with Mark Rossiter friendship don't count a lick against a debt of more'n a dollar and a half. Yeste-day a bunch of cowpokes from up around Junction City drove a thousand head of prime cows through Rossiter, and Mark stood on the bank steps and beamed on 'em, rubbin' his hands. Reckon he's already figgered his profit on the deal."

"Those notes sure must have piled up."

"Forty thousand dollars' worth of 'em!"

"Wow! Why, it'll take the whole thousand head to pay that off."

"Accordin' to Rossiter it'll take more'n that. The Colonel deeded a strip of range a mile wide and six miles across to cover the balance."

Lance stared. "Rossiter took *land?* He must be a friend after all."

"Yeah. I can't figger it. What's he want with land?"

"Mebbe he's figgerin' on a bigger back yard for that town of his'n," observed Joe.

"He's figuring out something, you can bet on that," agreed Lance grimly.

"Feller, you said it," agreed Abner. "Them damn Yanks got somethin' cookin' and it smells like b'iled skunk to me. Dawggone it, I shore feel sorry for Nancy and the Colonel. They're proud as all getout and they'll take their medicine without whimperin', but I'll bet my new hat ag'in a wore-out curry comb that somewhere along the line they're bein' rooked."

The old man stayed for supper and they discussed the matter off and on during the evening. They sensed something wrong but couldn't put their fingers on it. Certainly Rossiter wasn't going in for ranching or he would have kept the cattle. The land was just about worthless for anything else but building lots and that Rossiter would expand over an area of an additional six square miles was inconceivable.

Abner had not seen hair or hide of Ben Clark, nor had anybody else he had questioned. The guards who were constantly watching the Clark and Pendleton house had nothing but negative reports. Ben had either skipped the country or had crawled into a hole and pulled the hole in after him.

"We'll keep watching for him," said Lance. "If he does come back it'll be just too bad. Bud Kelly spends all his spare time cleaning and oiling his .45 and he'll drop Ben on sight."

The guard who was watching the town made a report. "Somebody's buildin' fence across the valley this side of town. And there's a bunch of surveyors runnin' lines. Big fat feller with a brown beard is givin' directions."

"Fence? About a mile this side of town?"

"Just about a mile, I reckon."

"Hm-m. As the novels say, the plot thickens. The gentleman with the beard is Mark Rossiter and the land he is fencing is a strip he got from the Pendletons for some notes he held. We've been wondering what he wanted the land for; now we'll be wondering why the fence."

"Mebbe he's struck oil," drawled Joe.

"He's found something that'll pay off, and it's beginning to look to me as though he knew it was there all the time."

Joe flashed him a quick look. "Figger he took land for the balance of them notes because he'd been anglin' to get it all along, huh?"

"Maybe. Otherwise, why the fence all of a sudden?"

They were kept busy working cattle, venting brands and burning on their ACC, but the thing kept bothering Lance. There was a question he wanted to ask that nobody but the Pendletons could answer and he found himself wishing that he had made it possible for those neighborly visits which Nancy had mentioned on the occasion of her first call. So far as the Pendletons were concerned his scheme of vengeance had boomeranged sadly.

He summoned his courage and rode over one evening, telling himself that the most they could do was run him off the spread. The buildings looked forlorn and there was but a single horse in the corral. Dusk had fallen and there was a light in the kitchen. He mounted the gallery and knocked on the front door.

Nancy opened it and he took off his hat and said, "Good evening, Miss Pendleton. May I have a moment with your grandfather?"

"Grandfather isn't at home, Mr. Jones." Her voice was cool, impersonal.

"Perhaps you'll talk with me then?"

"If it's quite necessary. Will you come in or would you rather sit out here?"

"I'd like it out here, if you don't mind." He stood until she had seated herself, then sat down and put his hat over his knees. She was wearing Levi's and wool shirt and had gathered her warm brown hair together with a blue ribbon. She looked tired and a sudden pity stirred him.

He said quietly, "The loss of your cattle to the bank is common knowledge, so perhaps you'll let me say I'm sorry that you found it necessary to part with them."

"Sorry?" Her voice was skeptical. "I should think you'd be glad. You came back, didn't you, to drag the mighty from their places and to humble the proud Pendletons? I think that's how you put it."

He felt his cheeks burning. "That was my purpose, yes. It seems childish now. I've been thinking of it a lot since that evening you asked me for range. You said something then that sort of jarred me. Perhaps after all it was my ego which drove me rather than any real desire to avenge the death of my grandfather on the Pendletons. It's bothered me all the more because I can't be certain in my own mind. All that I can think of now is that if it hadn't been for that miserable fence of mine you wouldn't have to sacrifice your cattle."

She said calmly, her voice still cool. "It would have happened in any event. The plain truth is that we didn't realize how much we were borrowing. The loans were for me—my schooling, my clothes, the unbelievable cost of maintaining the front expected of a Pendleton and a great many foolish expenditures on my part. I'm entirely to blame. As it is, we're quite satisfied with a smaller ranch and fewer cattle. Grandfather has been bearing the burden ever since the death of my father and the burden was just too great for old shoulders. Please don't feel sorry for us; we're going to be very happy, I assure you."

There it was; the proud Pendletons. Staunch and loyal, taking the whole blame on herself. He sat there trying to study her through the growing darkness. He saw indistinctly a chin proudly tilted, a head slightly cocked to one side, he felt the calm, impersonal scrutiny of violet eyes. He said slowly, "I wish you'd answer a question for me, Miss Pendleton. Has Mark Rossiter ever approached your grandfather with a proposal to buy the Stars and Bars or any part of it?"

She did not answer for a moment, and when she did her words were carefully chosen. "Mr. Rossiter has never made an offer on his own behalf."

"On the behalf of another then?"

"Once. Three years ago. Grandfather refused to consider any offer at all."

"But Rossiter did make an offer on the behalf of another. Would you mind telling me who it was?"

"The name was not mentioned. Mr. Rossiter simply stated that he knew of a party who would be interested in buying if we cared to sell, and grandfather told him he would never sell the Stars and Bars while he was managing it."

Lance said, "Thank you very much," and got to his feet.

She rose also and he could feel her gaze upon him. "Why did you want to know this, Mr. Jones?"

"Because," he said slowly, "I have a peculiar hunch that you've been victimized by these friends of yours. If you have, I want to know it. The feeling that my desire for revenge was childish and petty doesn't extend to them. They were the ones who detained me that night; if anybody contributed to my grandfather's death, it was they."

"So you're still determined to punish."

"Those people, yes. Doubly so if they have been using you to further some clever Yankee scheme."

"And why this sudden interest in our welfare?"

"Because," he heard himself say, "I'm in love with you."

He caught her quick gasp of surprise. She said sharply, "Mr. Jones!"

He was appalled now; appalled and bewildered. "I know. I'm a damned fool. I hadn't intended telling you; the fact is, I didn't realize it myself until just now. You don't need to tell me how hopeless it is; you'll always see me as you saw me that night, wearing those ridiculous clothes, with my hair plastered down and that hillbilly glow on my cheeks. Just forget that I mentioned it. Good night."

He turned away abruptly and went down the steps; he vaulted into his saddle without checking his momentum and his spurs bit as he hit the saddle so that the leap of his horse was but a continuation of his own motion. His jaws were set and he was cursing himself under his breath. The words had come out without any conscious effort and he had spoken the truth. He knew now that he had loved her from the moment she had stepped around the rocks that evening and had said, "Well! What are you doing here?"

He knew now that his desire to punish her had come from the fact that he had appeared ridiculous in her eyes. He wanted to justify himself, to be able to say, "You laughed at me then; look at me now." Maybe his hatred of the others sprang from the same source; but if they had victimized her and her grandfather he'd make them pay and there wouldn't be any question in his mind as to whether or not they deserved it.

Now that he had dragged out the truth and spread it where both he and Nancy could see it, he was filled with a burning desire to help her. There had been five thousand head of cattle on the Stars and Bars at one time, but he could not believe that half the herd had been spirited away in a single year. That meant that the thefts had gone on over a period of years and, since he was sure the Colonel would leave such matters as tallying to the crew, that crew had falsified the count to cover up their thefts. Well, cattle wearing such a conspicuous brand as the Stars and Bars could be traced, and by God he was going to do some tracing.

Joe was in bed when he reached the *hacienda* but he talked it over with him after breakfast. He explained his sudden change of heart. "The ones I'm really out to get are that bunch in Rossiter, and I have a hunch that the rustling of Pendleton cattle is somehow tied up with Rossiter's scheme to get the land. It had to be fixed so that Pendleton couldn't pay off the whole debt in cows. Tracing the rustling to Mark Rossiter would give me the hold on him that I want."

"Also," drawled Joe, "the lady was very fair."

Lance felt his cheeks warm. He set his jaws and glared at Joe. "All right; so what?"

"So what? Hell, feller, nothin' except that if you've gone and fallen in love with Nancy Pendleton you've done just about the most sensible thing a feller could do. I've been carryin' out your orders, but I'll admit my heart ain't been in it; now if you're workin' for her instead of against her I'm with you every jump in the road."

Lance grinned. "If you wish, you may shake the hand of a big damned fool."

Lance set out that morning on his attempt to trace the Stars and Bars cattle. He forded the creek at the point where the stolen cattle had crossed, topped a slight rise and found a shallow trench, now overgrown with grass, which had been at one time the bed of the creek. It meandered diagonally across the valley and through a narrow gap in the hills, eventually

155

reaching another valley through which ran a large river. The creek had originally emptied into this.

Lance followed the old creek bed into the second valley and camped on the bank of the river to eat his dinner, then found a trail which led westward and kept to it until, late in the afternoon, he sighted the buildings of a ranch.

He rode up to the house and the owner came out to welcome him and invite him to supper. While they were eating, Lance told his host that he came from the other valley and mentioned the Stars and Bars.

"I know where it is," said the rancher, whose name was Barlow, "but I ain't never been over there. Bought a small bunch of Stars and Bars three-year-olds just a couple of months ago."

"You've met Colonel Pendleton, then?"

"Nope. Feller named Clark delivered and collected for the critters. He stopped in one day for dinner and we got to talkin' cattle and he said the Stars and Bars were cuttin' down and had some prime three-year-old cows and steers they'd sell at a fair price. I ordered fifty head and Clark came along with the crew that delivered them and collected. It was a good buy for me; I'll use the she stuff for breedin' and then sell 'em for beef and the steers will bring me a nice profit."

"Clark gave you a bill of sale, I suppose."

"Sure. Signed by Pendleton's agent; feller named—can't call his name now. Wait a minute; I got that bill of sale right handy."

He got a paper from his desk and handed it over to Lance. "Ordman; that's the name. Jacob Ordman."

Lance scanned the bill of sale briefly. It covered a mixed herd of three-year-olds bearing the Stars and Bars brand, price one thousand dollars. It was dated July 9 and was signed by Jacob Ordman.

Barlow urged Lance to stay overnight but he said he had to be pushing on. He followed the river trail until darkness set in, then made camp. At noon of the next day he sighted another ranch house and had dinner with the owner. This man was named Richmond and he too had purchased some cattle from Ben Clark. The bill of sale, signed by Ordman, covered forty head of three-year-olds, cows and steers, price eight hundred dollars, dated August 12.

Lance started back for home satisfied that he had enough information to start with. If these two transactions were legitimate ones, Ordman would have reported them to Colonel Pendleton or would have a record of them. If he had not accounted for these ninety head of prime cattle they'd have the goods on him and Ben Clark.

He reached the ACC in the evening and found Abner and Joe in the kitchen eating supper. Joe asked him what luck he'd had and he told of the sale of three-year-olds to Barlow and Richmond.

"The Colonel sellin' three-year-olds at that price?" scoffed Abner. "Not in ten million years. Ben stole 'em, but the whole passel of 'em was in on it. They was busy as hell makin' sure the Colonel wouldn't have enough stock to settle them notes."

"Ordman had the authority to sell them; before we can pin anything on him we've got to show that he didn't record the sales or report them to the Colonel. What's new at Rossiter, Abner?"

"Plenty. The Rossiter Development Company has been foaled and is kickin' up its heels right merry. They's a big sign right outside of town on the ranch road sayin' that the Rossiter Development Comp'ny is offerin' acreage suitable for farmin' and guaranted to be fertile and well watered."

"Well watered? For six miles across the valley?"

"Yessir. Got a map painted on the sign showin' that six-by-one-mile strip divided into twenty-four quarter-sections. It shows the creek bein' diverted right and left to flow acrost the valley over the top row of quarter-sections and back ag'in over the second row and into the original channel. Every one of them quarter-sections will have water."

"So that's what they've been angling for! That's why they wanted that land. They'll parcel it out to farmers and soak them plenty. And Rossiter's bank will lend them money. The low-down swindlers!"

"Say it in a whisper, son," advised Abner bitterly, "or they'll sue you for slander. Ain't a danged thing illegal about it."

"The hell there isn't!" said Lance fiercely. "Rossiter approached the Colonel three years ago with an offer to buy and the Colonel turned him down flat. Then and there they planned to steal that land from him. They urged him to borrow money on mortgages, Ordman got himself appointed his agent, put a crooked crew on the spread and since then have been stealing from him so that he wouldn't be able to pay the notes when they were called. Twenty-five hundred head of stock at twenty dollars a head; that's fifty thousand dollars, and you can bet your bottom dollar the Colonel never saw a cent of it. And you sit there and tell me there's nothing illegal about it!"

"Prove it," said Abner calmly.

The fierceness died. "Yes; prove it. That's the rub. But we've got a start. If Ordman is asked for an accounting and fails to report those sales we've got him. We'll trace other sales until we have him tied in knots."

"The Colonel'll have to ask for that accountin'

and he still figgers Ordman is his friend. How you goin' to get around that?"

"I'll find a way. I've got to get Pendleton's confidence first."

He took his first step after supper. He rode over to the Stars and Bars and found Colonel Pendleton seated in his big chair on the gallery. Nancy was not in sight. As he mounted to the gallery the Colonel got up and said stiffly, "Good evening, Mr. Jones. What can I do for you, suh?"

"You can listen to me for a moment, sir, if you will."

The Colonel surveyed him with cool, keen eyes. "Will you be seated?"

Lance sat down and when the Colonel resumed his seat said slowly, "I rode over, Colonel, to return the five thousand dollars you paid me. My intention was to forward the money to the relatives of the man who was shot, but I find that he was an orphan with no near relatives living." He handed the Colonel an envelope containing the five thousand dollars in bank notes.

The Colonel cleared his throat and turned the envelope slowly over in his hands. For once he was at a loss. Lance went on, "I've also reconsidered the matter of grazing rights. Since the company will not be adding to its stock for some time there's no reason why you shouldn't use the range. My men will start removing the fence tomorrow."

The Colonel murmured, "You are very kind, Mr. Jones, but we are in no need of additional range now. I must admit, suh, that your estimate of the number of our cattle was better than mine." He sighed and shook his head. "I can't understand it."

"I'm afraid you sold off more stock than you realize, Colonel. I talked with two ranchers in the next valley who recently purchased some three-year-olds from the Stars and Bars."

"Three-year-olds?" The Colonel's voice was sharp. "Cows or steers?"

"Mixed. The bills of sale were signed by Jacob Ordman."

"He's my agent, suh; but he should have reported the sales to me."

"Probably an oversight," said Lance and got up. "I'll be moseying along, Colonel. And that fence is coming down, starting in the morning."

It was the Colonel who extended his hand. "Thank you again, Mr. Jones. I believe, suh, that you are a Southerner?"

"Born in Tennessee, Colonel. Right next door to your folks in Kentucky."

Pendleton's eyes brightened. "Neighbors, suh! Let us remain so. Please do us the honor of having dinner with us sometime."

Lance thanked him and rode away, the dusk settling about him. When he had covered a mile or so he heard the rapid drum of hoofbeats behind him and turned to look. A pony was galloping after him and on the pony was Nancy. He halted his horse and took off his hat as she pulled up before him.

She said, "Mr. Jones, I was in the front room when you talked with my grandfather. The window was open and I heard. Tell me about those sales."

He repeated what he had told the Colonel but went into further detail.

"The cattle were delivered by your crew under the supervision of Ben Clark. Ben collected for them and gave Ordman's bill of sale."

She was frowning. "Why did Mr. Ordman sell good stock like that?"

"Do you really want my opinion?"

"Yes, I do."

He told her bluntly what he thought: that the Rossiter Development Company had not been born in the last week or so but had had its inception three years ago; that her grandfather had been invited to borrow on mortgage notes and that their cattle had been rustled in order that he would be unable to meet those notes when payment was demanded. "In that way," he finished, "you were forced to deed over the land Rossiter wanted and that you refused to sell him. The very fact that he first offered to buy confirms that."

The violet eyes were troubled. "I just can't believe they'd do that."

"It's easy to prove or disprove. Ask Jacob Ordman for an accounting. Don't say anything about sales, just tell him that you're going to set up books for the ranch and need the information he has. If the sales to Barlow and Richmond on July 9 and August 12 are not recorded we can check further."

"I'll do it," she promised. "I hope you're mistaken; I'd rather lose the cattle than my faith in human nature. Goodnight, Mr. Jones."

She called on Ordman the next afternoon. She hadn't told her grandfather of her conversation with Lance because she did not want to worry him. Beneath the JACOB B. ORDMAN, Attorney at Law, on the office door was a placard which said VICE PRESIDENT AND TREASURER, ROSSITER DEVELOPMENT CO. Ordman greeted her with a stiffness which had been entirely missing in the past.

She came to the point at once. "Mr. Ordman, I've decided to set up a bookkeeping system at the ranch and I'd like to have all the records pertaining to the Stars and Bars since grandfather employed you as manager."

"The records?" Ordman frowned at her. "My dear girl, I couldn't possibly turn them over to anybody but your grandfather."

"It is my ranch, Mr. Ordman, and I wouldn't

ask for them if I weren't sure of grandfather's consent."

He shook his head. "Colonel Pendleton must make the request himself. Have him come in and I'll gladly turn everything over to him."

She wasted no time in argument. She said stiffly, "We'll be here first thing in the morning. Good evening, Mr. Ordman."

Anger stirred her as she rode homeward, an anger which was intensified when she read the bold sign which stood by the road. Was Lance right? Was the whole thing a clever conspiracy from the very beginning? On the morrow she would know. If Ordman's records failed to show those two transactions she would be morally certain that they had been victimized.

That night there was a fire in Rossiter. Due to the vigilance of Marshal Dave Schultz it did not spread. Schultz, patrolling the town shortly before midnight, saw the glow in Ordman's office, shouted an alarm, then broke into the building. A bucket brigade was quickly formed and the damage was confined to the interior of the building. Ordman's office furniture was blistered and charred and all papers and records were destroyed, including those concerned with his management of the Pendleton ranch.

Nancy and her grandfather learned about the fire when they drove to town the next morning. She had persuaded the Colonel to ask for an accounting without revealing her reason for wanting one. They found Ordman contemplating the scene of destruction and he explained that he had taken the records from the safe to check over and arrange in anticipation of the Colonel's visit and had left them on his desk. They had, alas! been totally destroyed.

Nancy watched him as he explained and thought she could detect an ironic glint in his eyes. She felt suddenly tired and dispirited. If these friends of theirs were crooked, what chance did a young girl and an old man have against them? The fire, she felt, was no coincidence. Lance had been right in his suspicion of Ordman, but the proof he needed was gone.

She hardly heard what he said after that, and it wasn't until they were on their way home that she remembered his saying something about starting for the East that very day. She asked, "Grandfather, what was it Mr. Ordman said about going East?"

The old man spoke calmly enough, but there was a tinge of bitterness in his voice. "He's going East, my dear, to escort the first of the settlers to our valley. It seems that we are to be subjected to another Yankee invasion."

Six

That same morning Lance put his crew at work removing the fence. He was working with them when Nancy came riding up. He went to meet her and she told him of the fire which had destroyed the records. The proof he needed of Ordman's guilt was now gone. He gave her a tight grin. "Sure was a coincidence, that fire."

"I wish I could believe it was. It's so hard—"

"I know. We'll just have to sit tight and wait for them to make a slip." He didn't feel as hopeful as he spoke. He asked, "How are you fixed for help? I can spare a few hands if you need them."

"Thank you. Grandfather found three of our old hands and hired them." She glanced along the line where the fence had been. "You've been very generous, Mr. Jones, but it really wasn't necessary to take down the fence."

"You never can tell. Someday I hope to see the Stars and Bars right back where it used to be."

She gave him a faint smile and rode away.

That evening he rode by a circuitous route through the trees to the place where a man was stationed day and night to watch the Clark and Pendleton houses against Ben Clark's return. He took his regular trick with the men and would be on the job all night. Bud Kelly would relieve him at dawn. The man on watch reported nothing doing and headed for the ranch, and Lance picked up the field glasses and took a sweeping look around the country.

He studied the Pendleton house for a while, noticing the three cowhands watering the corral stock, then caught a fleeting glimpse of Nancy as she moved about the kitchen. He could not see the front of the house but guessed the Colonel would be seated in his favorite chair on the gallery. Then he moved the glasses to the right and picked up the Clark house.

There was no sign of life for awhile except the horse in the corral; then the elder Clark came out and stood for some minutes looking towards the ACC buildings. The dusk was deepening. Satisfied that nobody was in sight, Clark went to the corral, slipped a halter on his horse and led the animal to the rear of the house and tied him close to the kitchen doorway. His movements were furtive. He got his rig and saddled up, then went into the house.

Lance waited, the glasses on the house. The darkness deepened and presently the house and its surroundings were swallowed in the gloom. He got out a memorandum book and a pencil and scribbled a note. *Clark is going some-where. I'm going to follow him. Lance.* He put the note on a rock and weighed it down with a stone, then, taking the glasses with him, went back to where he had left his horse, mounted and rode quickly down the slope. At the fringe of trees back of the buildings he left the horse and went ahead on foot to the rear of the house. Here he crouched down to wait.

Two hours passed before he heard the creak of hinges as the door was opened. There was no light in the house but he caught Clark's dark shadow as he came through the doorway. He was carrying a bulky object which he proceeded to tie behind his saddle. He untied the horse, mounted and rode away.

Lance got his horse and followed, walking and leading the animal, keeping Clark in sight by the light of the stars. Clark rode slowly for about a mile, then crossed the creek at the ford and dropped out of sight in the old creek bed. Lance mounted his horse and followed him knowing that Clark could not observe him after he had entered the depression. Clark led him clear across the valley and through the gap.

The moon came up as they were passing through the hills. Clark left the dried creek bed before it reached the river and turned east. Lance, on his previous trip to this second valley, had turned west. Almost at once they were ascending into the hills, following a well-traveled trail. It was close to dawn when Clark rode over the top of a ridge and down a slope which led to what Lance judged to be a grassy basin. On the far side, a mile or so away, the fading moonlight fell on a small cluster of buildings. Clark rode straight across the basin towards these; Lance remained at the top of the slope, watching.

Clark dismounted at a corral and stripped his horse. He unstrapped the bundle and went into the largest of the buildings; a light showed briefly then was extinguished. Lance found a bit of rimrock with a dry wash cutting it and rode his horse into it, loosened the cinches and tied him to a stunted tree. He got the glasses and stretched out on the ground.

Dawn broke and men came out of the bunkhouse to make their way to what Lance guessed was the mess shack. Half an hour passed and they came out again and went to the corral for their horses. He counted eight of them. They mounted and rode to a small fenced pasture containing thirty or forty head of cattle. The herd was shaped up for a drive, point and drag men and flankers moved into their places and the whole column headed across the basin. Lance watched through the glasses as they approached, headed into the trail by which Clark had descended, climbed slowly upward and passed to his left. He saw that the cattle wore the Stars and Bars brand and that the men who drove them were Buck Borden and his bunch.

The cattle gone, Lance transferred his attention back to the cabin. After a while the front door opened and two men came out. One was the elder Clark, the other was Ben. There was a bench outside the cabin and the two men sat down on it. Lance saw them make and light cigarettes and guessed that they intended to remain there for some time. He got his horse and made his way around the circumference of the basin until he reached a point directly behind the cabin.

He found a path which angled down the slope to the rear of sheds and corrals and descended this, keeping a wary eye on the house and buildings. At the bottom he tied his horse behind a shed and moved across the open space to the rear door.

He stood there for a moment listening, heard no sound and opened the door. He was looking through an untidy kitchen and through a doorway into a larger room and then beyond that through the open front doorway and the basin now green and bright under the sun. He stepped into the kitchen and tiptoed across the floor, intending to surprise the Clarks on the bench outside.

The elder Clark's footsteps must have been

muffled by the soft grass for Lance was given no warning whatever. The old man just appeared suddenly in the front doorway, halted to stare for the space of a heartbeat, then snatched out his gun.

Lance's reaction was instinctive. He did not pride himself on his skill and speed with a Colt but now his life was at stake and he yanked out the gun, tilted up the muzzle and fired from the hip. The distance was not more than fifteen feet and a blind man could not have missed such a large target. Clark dropped his gun, staggered forward a few steps, then collapsed on the floor. Instantly Lance wheeled and three running strides took him to the back doorway and a leap carried him through it.

His brain functioned swiftly while he acted; he wheeled to his left and sprinted around the corner and along the side of the cabin, running silently and ducking below the window level. He wheeled around the front corner, his Colt levelled. The bench was empty.

There was no porch; without checking his speed he ran the three steps to the front doorway and wheeled into it. Ben Clark was crouched over the body of his father, his gun covering the rear doorway. He heard Lance's step and started to turn, and as he moved Lance called sharply, "Hold it!"

Ben got around far enough to see him, then

froze. Lance said, "Drop the gun," Ben swore and let the weapon fall.

Lance said, "Back up," and when Ben halted in a corner of the room he circled warily, stooped and snatched up the guns Ben and his father had dropped. He tossed them through the front doorway, made Ben face the wall with his hands above his head, and patted him for other weapons. He found a clasp knife and pocketed it. He said, "Take a look at your father."

Ben turned slowly, gave him a glare, then knelt beside his father. He probed around for a minute then growled, "You hit him in the shoulder; smashed the collar bone."

Lance said, "Fix him up," and followed Ben into the kitchen and watched while he got hot water from the stove and found some clean flour sacks. When the wound had been bandaged and the old man laid on a bunk, Lance said, "Sit down; we're going to have a talk."

Ben sat on a chair and Lance dropped to the edge of a bunk, the Colt in his lap. He said, "One of the Stars and Bars men told us it was you who shot Slim Hawkins. That makes you a murderer."

"It was self-defense," blurted Ben. "You can't prove different."

"Slim had a friend named Bud Kelly; Kelly won't need any proof. He's sworn he'll shoot you on sight and he'll do it. Tell me what I want to know and I'll turn you over to the law at Junction City before Kelly knows I've got you. Refuse to talk, or try lying to me and I'll take you back to the ACC and let events take their course."

Ben's lips curled in a sneer. "You can't bluff me, Jones. My men are close at hand and you'll never get me back to the ACC."

"Your men," Lance told him, "started out on a cattle drive and won't be back very soon. They're probably delivering another bunch of Stars and Bars cattle, giving Ordman's bill of sale to make it look legal."

He caught the start Ben gave and went on. "Over a period of three years you and Ordman have stolen twenty-five hundred head of stock. I can even give you dates and names. On July 9 you delivered fifty three-year-olds to a man named Barlow, and on August 12 you delivered forty more to Richmond. You collected the money for them and gave them Ordman's bills of sale. But all Ordman's got to do is deny ever signing those bills of sale and you're up against it for rustling and forgery."

Ben's eyes flamed and he leaped to his feet. "He's pinning it on me? Why, the lousy skunk!"

"Do you think he's going to put his neck in a noose on your account? You ought to know him better than that. Sit down."

Ben slowly sank into the chair. He opened his mouth to speak and ended by licking dry lips with his tongue. Lance went on, "I'm gradually getting the goods on the whole bunch of Rossiter rats. I know those cattle were rustled to keep Pendleton from meeting forty thousand dollars' worth of notes and to force him to deed Rossiter the land he needed for his Development Company."

Ben was staring at him in wonderment. Lance said in that same dry, level tone, "You'd be surprised how much I know. I know that Rossiter and the rest cooked up that scheme three years ago, planning to get the land, divert the creek to water it, and sell it in small chunks to farmers. They made you a party to the scheme so that you would rustle the cattle for them, but now you've done your share and they'll throw you to the wolves in order to keep their own hands clean."

Ben said again, "The lousy skunks!"

"You didn't think that four years ago when you helped chase another boy named Jones out of Rossiter."

Ben gave a start. He peered keenly at Lance. "You *that* Jones?"

"Yes. I told you I'd come back and that you'd all be sorry, so under ordinary circumstances I'd hand you over to Bud Kelly without any qualms whatever. But I need proof of what I know; proof that'll stand up in a court of law. And you can furnish that proof by testifying against

174

Rossiter and his gang. I'm giving you that chance; tell the truth and I'll hand you over to the law instead of to Bud Kelly. If you can get away with self-defense you won't hang."

A weak voice came from the other bunk. "Tell him, Ben. I said from the start them polecats would look after their own hides and to hell with you."

Ben stared hard at Lance for a few seconds then said, "All right, I'll tell you. And I'll repeat the story before the proper authorities. The plan was hatched three years ago just like you said, with the Colonel being urged to borrow and with Ordman his manager to make it easier. Ordman got rid of the old Stars and Bars crew and put Buck Borden and his boys on the spread. I was to rustle young stock, fetch 'em over here and use 'em for breeding, since that brand couldn't be altered. When I'd bred them I was to sell them off in small bunches with Ordman covering me with bills of sale. The calves were branded with my Circle C and became my property; the money from the sales went to pay Buck and the boys and Ordman. The idea was, like you said, to reduce the Colonel's stock so that he wouldn't have enough to raise the money for the notes. The tally sheets were doctored to show a permanent herd of five thousand. When the showdown came, the Colonel would be accused of obtaining loans on collateral that didn't exist and would be forced to deed over the land to square up. Rossiter, Ordman, Bennett, Taylor, Dunn and myself were in it. The whole damned bunch of them is guilty of criminal conspiracy and they can be hooked up with the rustling, too."

Lance got up. "We'll make your father comfortable and leave food and water where he can reach it. Buck Borden can take care of him when they come back from their drive."

When the elder Clark had been attended to, both men went out and Lance watched while Ben caught up and saddled his horse. They set out for Junction City which, Ben told him, could be reached without passing through the valley or the town of Rossiter. Ben led the way and Lance followed, his sixgun ready. He was elated with his success and was determined that Ben should not escape; Ben's testimony would convict Rossiter and his bunch, would restore land and cattle to Pendleton and obliterate the Rossiter Development Company.

Ben's plea of self-defense would not hold water. The Avenger crew could swear that Slim had been shot at close quarters and that his gun was still in its holster when his body was found.

They topped the rim of the basin and followed the trail to the point where the old creek bed joined the river. Here Ben took the path which Lance had followed to the Barlow and Richmond ranches. The road twisted and turned, following the river which in turn conformed to the contour of the ground, and at times they passed through groves of trees as the trail curved close to the river. They emerged abruptly from a thicket of pinoaks and Ben, in the lead, suddenly stiffened in the saddle and jerked his horse to a halt.

Lance, instantly alert, brought up his Colt thinking that it was Buck Borden and his crowd that Ben had sighted. He quickly swerved his horse in order to see beyond Ben. A horseman had leaped his mount from behind some trees to block the road. He sat his mount like a rock, his Colt pointed at Ben, and behind the glinting barrel Lance saw a hard, drawn face with lips tightly compressed and eyes blazing through slitted lids. It was Bud Kelly.

Lance shouted, but he was too late. Blending with his voice came the heavy boom of the Colt. Ben rose in his stirrups as though about to leap, then folded up like a wet sack, slumped over his saddle horn and slipped sideways to the ground.

Ben Clark was dead, there was no doubt of that. And with him had died Lance's hope of pinning criminal charges on Rossiter and his bunch. Sitting there gazing down at the still body he was momentarily overcome with a sick feeling of failure which amounted almost to physical nausea. Following this came a wave of hot anger for the man who had taken Ben's life and he looked into the stony face of Bud Kelly and said, "Damn you to hell, Kelly!"

Kelly said, "I swore I'd down him on sight and I did. He was a dirty murderer and you know it. What's your beef?"

The anger passed and the sick feeling came back. Lance said, "I was taking him to Junction City to tell a story that would have put Rossiter and his dirty gang behind the bars. And the law would have hanged Ben Clark until he was every bit as dead as your bullet made him."

Kelly said sullenly, "I said I'd get him. I ain't sorry."

Lance groaned. "Pack him somewhere on his horse and bury him. Keep your eyes open for Buck Borden's gang; they drove some cows over this trail and they'll be back."

"I seen 'em. I found your note and figgered maybe the old man would lead you to Ben. It was too good a chance to pass up. I follered but never did catch up with you. I turned west instead of east and spent the night ridin' around. This mornin' I heard cattle comin' and slipped back into the trees. I recognized Borden and figgered they was workin' for Ben. I started back the way they'd come and then I heard you comin' and ducked again. Ben rode out of the trees first and when I seen him I didn't wait to see anybody else."

Lance nodded his understanding and started

back for the ACC. He tried to shake off his depression by fast riding but it was no go. Ben had talked because he thought his life was at stake; it was doubtful if Lance could get the evidence he needed from one of the others because he possessed no lever with which to pry the truth from them.

He reached the ranch late that afternoon and told Joe what had happened while they ate supper. "Bud Kelly sure killed two birds with one shot—Ben Clark and my hopes."

"He sure messed up the deal, Lance, but you can't hardly blame him. Ben was a dirty killer and Slim was Bud's friend."

"I know. But now I've got to find some other way of pinning the goods on Rossiter, and I don't for the life of me see how it can be done. All we can do now is sit tight and watch."

They sat tight and watched for a month. They rode to Ben's hill ranch the next day and swept into the basin prepared for war; but if Buck Borden and his crew had returned, Ben's father had certainly warned them. The old man was moving around under his own power, his arm in a sling. Lance told him of Ben's death and he took it with stony calm; but hate smouldered in his eyes and Lance knew he would never get any help from him.

Lance said, "We're driving these cows back to the valley and we're going to vent the

Circle C and put Stars and Bars on them. My advice to you is to go back to your own spread and work the Circle C stuff there."

They started rounding up the next day and by the end of the week they entered the valley driving over a thousand head of cattle, calves, yearlings, two-year-olds and a fair number of older stock still wearing the Stars and Bars. They drove them across Pendleton range to within a quarter of a mile of the house where they were met by Nancy and the Colonel and their three cowboys. The Colonel's eyes were shining and there was hope and wonder on Nancy's face. She pulled her pony to a halt and cried, "Lance, what is it?"

He felt a little thrill; she had called him by his first name. He explained quickly but did not mention Ordman's name in connection with the rustling. That would come later. With the aid of the three cowhands, the Circle C cattle were segregated and put in holding corrals for rebranding, and those still wearing the Stars and Bars were permitted to scatter over the range.

When the work was finished the Colonel insisted that Lance return to their house for supper, and when Nancy added her plea to that of her grandfather Lance accepted. He washed up and went into the house to find Nancy awaiting him. She had shed her work clothes for a flowered house dress and her brown curls hung in a warm cluster over one shoulder.

Aunt Betsy had outdone herself and the meal was one to be remembered; but more pleasing to Lance than the excellent food was the gaiety of Nancy and the Colonel. After they had finished they sat on the gallery, and finally the Colonel shook hands with Lance and begged to be excused.

When they were alone in the starlight Nancy asked for and received a detailed report. He told her of Ben's confession and his offer to give evidence which would convict her one-time friends and of his death at the hands of Bud Kelly. She listened in grave silence and at the end uttered a tired sigh.

"It's so—so distressing, Lance. The loss of our land and cattle seems small beside the betrayal by our friends. And it looks as though we'll never be able to prove anything against them. They'll go on lording it over Rossiter—" She broke off, then said slowly, "I guess I shouldn't judge them; I've done my share of lording, too."

"When we're sixteen," he said quietly, "we don't stop to reason things out; we just follow the lead of those who are older and seem so much wiser."

He left shortly thereafter. He didn't want to spoil things, to wear out his welcome. He had told her that he loved her and that he had no hope for her affection in return; if ever he did win her regard she'd let him know in her own way.

The days passed and a fever of activity filled the end of the valley. Surveyors had finished subdividing the strip and an army of workers was busy digging new channels for the creek. Finally all that remained was the blast that would block the channel and remove the earth which would let the water flow across the valley.

The work was visible from the Pendleton side of the fence and Lance and Nancy rode down nearly every evening to watch its progress. Abner joined them occasionally and brought the latest news from town. A new cleanup drive was in progress with the citizens and taxpayers contributing liberally. The town council passed an ordinance requiring owners to paint their houses and stores and make all necessary repairs, and Dave Schultz was kept busy bullying and threatening to see that the work was done. People were muttering complaints because they felt that the work they did was for the benefit of the Development Company.

A stage line was organized and two Butterfield coaches purchased together with the necessary stock. A relay station was built halfway between Rossiter and Junction City and drivers and guards and stock tenders had been hired. The first official trip would bring Jacob Ordman and two coachloads of prospective buyers. There was to be a big celebration upon their arrival. Those who bought land would have their transportation paid and the generous banker, Mark Rossiter, would finance the cost of moving their families and household goods. At six percent interest, of course. And the bank would lend money to build homes and buildings and farm implements. Also at six percent.

"They'll git rich," said Abner bitterly. "Stinkin' rich. And the whole danged scheme is founded on crookedness. Lance, you gotta do somethin' about it." And Lance had worried and pondered and wondered what on earth he could do.

One day he heard the sound of blasting and rode down to the fence. The citizens of Rossiter were scattered over the newly laid-out sections of land. The creek had been diverted and from a slight elevation Lance could see the water slowly creeping right and left across the level valley floor through the channels which had been dug for it. North and south the water crawled across the twelve upper quarter-sections, then around the bends on the end ones and back to its original channel across the lower plots. It was a magnificent achievement, too magnificent to have had its foundation in treachery and theft and murder.

The idea occurred to him when he was riding gloomily homeward, and it was so simple and yet so appalling that he jerked his horse to an abrupt halt and sat staring out across the valley with wide eyes and thumping heart. It could be done! He could pull Rossiter and his bunch from their mighty places but in doing so he must pull the innocent with them. Unless—He tightened his lips and touched his horse with the spur. He would warn them first, give the innocent the chance to withdraw before catastrophe overtook them; if they failed to listen they would have nobody but themselves to blame.

He confided his inspiration to nobody, not even to Nancy. He spent a day riding about the valley, completing his plan. And the following morning Abner rode out to see him.

"Wal," the old man said tightly, "tomorry's the big day. Ordman and his pilgrims arrive around two in the afternoon. The town's decorated like it was the Fourth of July and they're buildin' a platform in front of the bank where Rossiter'll give 'em a welcomin' speech. Then him and the officers of the Rossiter Development Comp'ny'll lead the pee-rade out to the Garden of Eden. They'll have a big barbecue there and then troop back to town, where Rossiter'll spout some more, tellin' 'em what a wonderful world it's gonna be. And then they'll start takin' in the *dinero*."

"The spouting will be after the barbecue, eh? We'll be on hand."

At dinner the next day he told the crew they were free to ride to town and witness the celebration. "Personally, I don't want any of Rossiter's barbecued beef. All I ask of you boys is that you don't get drunk and that you'll be at that platform ready to back any play I make."

They knew the whole story of the swindle and Bud Kelly expressed the general opinion when he growled, "To hell with the barbecue, and to hell with gettin' drunk. I'll stick around and ride in with you."

There was a chorus of approval in which the whole crew joined.

They ate an early supper and rode away in a bunch, arriving in town shortly after dusk. The platform outside the bank building was brightly illuminated by kerosene flares, and upon it were the members of the Rossiter Development Company, all dressed in their Eastern finery. Benches had been placed directly in front of the stand and on these sat a dozen bright-eyed prospective buyers, all enthused about the well-watered and promising plots of land they had seen that evening. The townsfolk stood behind these benches and spilled around on the sides of the platform. Lance and his Texans sat their saddles in a quiet bunch behind the spectators.

Jacob Ordman had just introduced Mark Rossiter as "the father of this remarkable and profitable enterprise which will make our town the Flower of the West." There was a burst of applause from the prospects and a few *boos* from the citizens.

Rossiter arose with dignity, bowed his acknowledgement to Ordman and went into his act. The speech was a medley of the old tripe about the glorious future of Rossiter in general and themselves in particular. He painted a picture of prosperity and contentment, of fields of grain and fat stock and garden produce which would be swiftly transported by the Rossiter Stage and Freighting Company. He promised the Company's aid in the building of homes and the purchase of equipment, assuring them of long term loans by his bank. They ate it up. He hadn't mentioned the six percent. Or the various "handling charges."

"And now," he concluded, "you have seen the land, you have seen the clear, cool water flowing over it, you have realized how profitable this valley land can be made. We guarantee you a water supply which will never fail, water which can be carried by ditches to every square inch of your land. Mr. Ordman has quoted the price the Company is asking, a price which because of the productivity of the soil and the assurance of a continual water supply we consider very fair. Those of you who wish to avail yourselves of this wonderful opportunity may come to the platform and make the necessary arrangements with Mr. Ordman and myself."

He sat down amidst more enthusiastic applause from the prospects.

Lance said to Joe, "Here goes. Keep your eye on Dave Schultz," and stepped out of his saddle. Joe dismounted with him and moved quietly behind the marshal, who stood alertly in the rear, ready to squelch any hecklers. The Texans inched their horses through the crowd, and the townspeople, sensing a distraction, made way for them.

Lance slipped quickly through the fringe of spectators and leaped up the steps to the platform just in advance of the eager purchasers. He halted them with upraised hand and said, "Just a moment, folks."

From the rear of the crowd came Dave Schultz's roar, "Git down from there, Jones!" and immediately after it Joe's sharp voice, "Shut your yap and stand hitched!"

Lance spoke to the men who were so eager to reach the platform. "Listen to me before you do something you're going to regret. The land you are anxious to buy is there and the cool, clear water is flowing over it; but that land and water was acquired by fraud, by theft, by trickery and by murder. The proof of this is being assembled and in time will be complete, but by then you will have invested your savings in land that will be worthless for farming. I give you my word for that. Mark Rossiter is a big frog in a little puddle, but he's not God. How can he promise you a continuous supply of water? I ask you for your own good to hold off, to wait. The land won't run away."

Rossiter came to his feet, face red, eyes blazing. "You infernal scoundrel!" he roared. "That's a pack of lies! I'll—"

A gun thundered and they saw Rossiter's hair stir as a bullet clipped it before thudding into the wall of the bank. But Kelly yelled, "Sit down!"

Rossiter promptly sat down, the flush drained from his face.

Lance said quietly, "Let him spout, Bud. I've said my say; I've warned these folks and what I've said is the truth, even though I'm in no position to prove it now. But I'll tell you one thing with all the assurance in the world: you'll never raise grain or produce on that land."

He turned abruptly and left the platform and now the applause came from the citizens of Rossiter. Somebody yelled, "That's tellin' 'em, cowboy!"

Rossiter was on his feet again, the angry color back in his face. "The man has told you a pack of lies! He's a troublemaker and was run out of town and forbidden to return. He's here tonight because he has a bunch of lawless Texans to back him. He has made slanderous charges and has admitted his inability to substantiate them. The land was acquired legally and the deed is on file in Junction City where you can examine it for yourselves. And I hereby make this public announcement: if you find the land to be other than we have represented it to be I will refund every cent you have invested and in addition furnish transportation to your homes in the East. Is that fair enough for you?"

The buyers, who had hesitated, now surged to the platform. Lance motioned to his Texans and mounted his horse. Joe reminded Dave Schultz that it would be extremely unhealthy to start anything and joined him. He said, "Well, it was a nice try, feller. But you'll never make the bluff stick."

"Won't I?" Lance was grinning and excitement showed in his eyes. "Just wait and see. That guarantee of Rossiter's did it, Joe. He's laid himself wide open and they can come back on him for any loss. Come on; we got a lot of work to do."

All twelve of the prospects paid their money and got their deeds to valley land. They had been momentarily jarred by Lance's accusations, but his failure to produce any proof convinced them that he was, as Rossiter had told them, a troublemaker who sought to hurt Rossiter and his friends by mudslinging. Rossiter's guarantee against loss finally decided them.

The citizens of Rossiter were more than willing to believe Lance. They had borne the contempt and intolerance of the Rossiter crowd, they had been assessed taxes for improvements, including the welcoming decorations and the speakers' platform, they had been bullied into buying paint for their houses and roofing for their sheds and had been compelled to apply it, and they didn't like it at all. They hoped that Lance could make good his bluff.

"The feller's got somethin' up his sleeve," the storekeeper, Hank Wetherby, confided to his friends. "He knows somethin'. And them damn' Yanks *are* a bunch of crooks, no denyin' that. One'll get you five that Jones makes his brags good."

There were no takers.

The following day Jacob Ordman visited the hill ranch of Ben Clark in order to collect his cut on recent cattle sales and was brought up to date on developments by old man Clark. Ben was dead, the Stars and Bars cattle had been restored to their owners and Buck Borden and his bunch had taken to petty rustling and occasional highway robbery. Ordman, dismayed and a bit panicky, called the officers of the company together and passed on the information given him by Clark. They found the news disturbing.

"I wonder," said Leander Taylor worriedly, "how much Ben told the fellow."

Rossiter said, "From the way Jones spoke last night I imagine Ben told him everything. At the same time he admits that he has no proof, which would indicate that there was no witness to the conversation. Without a witness Jones is helpless. Ben is dead; we can blame the cattle thefts on him and Jacob can swear that his signatures on the bills of sale were forged. No, gentlemen, Jones can do nothing but make a nuisance of himself. But even a nuisance is irritating. Jacob, I think you should have a talk with Schultz."

"I'll see him at once," promised Ordman.

The others nodded grim approval. They had invested all their money in the scheme and L. Jefferson Jones was the only threat to the safety of that investment. His eradication was entirely desirable so long as the eradicating was accomplished by somebody else.

"How about Buck Borden and his men?" Bennett wanted to know.

"They took their orders from Ben; they know nothing of our part in it."

"I was thinking that it might be a good idea to have them handy in the event of another Texan invasion. I think we ought to hire them and deputize them. This Jones fellow was ordered out of town and we should be in a position to make our orders stick."

"You're quite right," approved Rossiter. "Jacob, see to it. You can probably contact them through old man Clark."

So Lance's doom was duly sealed and the protection of the town assured and the members of the Rossiter Development Company went their several ways with untroubled consciences.

Ordman sent for Dave Schultz and talked with him in his office. He said, "Schultz, you told this Jones fellow what would happen to him if he showed up in town and he came right back and made a monkey of you. What are you going to do about it?"

Dave scowled. "I said I'd get that jigger and I sure enough will."

"I'm glad to hear that. I'll give you a warrant for his arrest. He'll resist, of course, and that'll make the shooting legal."

Schultz looked doubtful. "You ain't askin' me to go out there and take him away from them Texans, are you?"

"You'll take him when he's alone. Fit yourself out with enough supplies to last a week and ride out to the Clark place. The old man's away and you can make yourself at home. Stay in the house and watch from the windows. Now that Jones has returned the Pendleton cattle he probably pays them a visit now and then. When he goes there some evening you can cut across the range and get him on his way home. It should be easy."

So Dave purchased the necessary supplies, hired a pack horse to carry them, and rode out to the Clark place that night. He did his riding before the moon came up and he did a lot of watching and listening to make sure that nobody else was abroad. He offsaddled and unpacked in the darkness and put the horses in the corral. The fact that he must leave them in plain view disturbed him, but he had to have his mount handy at all times and one horse in the corral would be just as bad as two. He decided that if anybody noticed them they would think old man Clark had come home and let it go at that.

He was up before dawn and set about cooking enough grub to last him the day before it was light enough for anybody to see smoke from the chimney; then he ate breakfast, set a tub of water within reach of the horses and tossed some hay into the corral. That done, he pulled a big chair up to a window and settled himself to watch.

In the distance he saw the Avenger crew ride to the creek and ford it to be hidden from his sight by the trees along the stream. He didn't see them again until evening, when they rode in for their suppers. He wondered vaguely what kind of work kept them busy on the far side of the creek.

His watching bore fruit the following evening. He was seated at the window eating a cold supper when he saw a horseman approaching from the direction of the ACC. He had no field glasses, but the rider passed within a quarter of a mile of the house and he recognized Jones. He saw Jones, a speck in the distance by that time, ride into the Pendleton yard.

He gobbled the rest of his supper, excitement gripping him. He had thought it all out and knew just what he must do. Regardless of the route Jones took in returning, he would be certain to strike the trail which paralleled the creek, and he was almost certain to strike it before he reached the ford. The ford, therefore, was the place to waylay him.

As soon as it was sufficiently dark to hide his movements, Dave went out, walked down his horse and saddled him. He mounted and struck out across the range, heading for the ford. When he reached the gap in the trees he rode on past it and took his station in the shadows. He drew his gun and tested its action. He was ready.

Lance sat on the Stars and Bars gallery talking with Nancy and the Colonel. It was just a neighborly visit. He liked Pendleton and he was in love with Nancy, although he had never touched on that since the day he had blurted out his confession. She must learn to know him first, form a genuine liking for him before he could hope to kindle the spark of love. So they chatted about inconsequential things and finally the Colonel bade them goodnight and went to his room.

Nancy said abruptly, "There's somebody over at the Clark house."

He was surprised. "You mean that old man Clark has come home?"

"I don't know. Somehow I don't think so. There are two horses in the corral but nobody ever comes out of the house during the daytime. This afternoon I rode over pretending to count our stock; somebody had set a tub of water where the horses could get at it and had tossed some hay into the corral. Whoever's inside the house is keeping pretty quiet about it."

"Did you mention it to your grandfather?"

"No, and I didn't say anything to the boys. I thought I'd tell you first."

"It *is* peculiar. Maybe the old man came home and his wound is infected and keeps him in bed. I'll ride over tomorrow and see."

They left it at that, but the thing stuck in his mind after he had told her goodnight and headed across the range towards the creek road. He did not believe that Clark had returned; a more logical explanation was that somebody had been posted there to watch the Pendleton ranch, or—remembering his speech of three nights before and the fury it had kindled in Rossiter— himself. And the only reason for watching him that he could think of was for the opportunity of catching him alone on the range.

The thought caused him to jerk his horse to a sudden halt and to sit there listening and peering over the dark range. He heard nothing unusual, saw nothing; but the feeling of impending danger impelled him to draw his gun before he rode on.

He told himself that he was being silly, but that strange premonition persisted. He reached the road which ran along the creek and redoubled his vigilance; and because he suddenly realized that the dark fringe of trees would make an excellent ambush and that anybody lying in wait for him would expect him to use this trail, he decided to cross at the ford and take to the range on the far side of the creek. He reached the gap a few minutes later, wheeled his horse and sent it splashing to the other side.

It was this move which forced Dave Schultz's hand. He was standing tense, his gun rising to cover the approaching horseman when the rider swung suddenly towards the creek and was instantly swallowed by the shadows. The next moment Dave heard the splash of water as Lance crossed the stream.

Dave turned and leaped on his horse, resolved to settle the thing now. On the open range Jones's figure would be visible in the starlight and if he followed swiftly enough he could get in a shot at close range. One shot, he felt sure, would be sufficient.

He spurred through the gap in the trees and splashed his horse through the creek. He spurred up the low bank, then felt his horse plunge into the shallow trench which had once been the creek bed. He had not known about the old bed and instinctively he reined in his horse. He heard the pound of hoofbeats ahead of him, temptingly close and hastily spurred in pursuit.

About five heartbeats later he felt arms go around him and fasten like the tentacles of an octopus. Had it actually been an octopus he couldn't have been more startled. A weight was dragging at him; it was too heavy to shake off. Dave snatched at the saddle horn, missed it and was torn from the saddle.

He fought then, fought desperately. Vaguely through his subconscious mind flashed an explanation. Jones had known he was being followed, had dropped off his horse while it was running and then had leaped upon him as he passed.

The fall had jarred him but he still clung to his gun. He tried now to bring it to bear on his opponent, but Jones had gripped his wrist with iron fingers. They struggled fiercely, Dave twisting his hand and moving his arm in frantic attempts to loosen the grip. Lance got his other hand on the one which held the gun and tightened down, and at the same time Dave gave a violent twist of his wrist. His thumb was on the hammer and the pressure drew it back. The next instant the hammer slipped from beneath his thumb and there was a flash and a roar as the weapon was discharged.

Lance struggled for a moment more before he realized that Dave was no longer resisting. He was partly blinded by the flame from the gun and the sting of powder burns was on his cheek. But Dave had suddenly gone limp. Lance disentangled himself and got to his knees, panting. He struck a match and took one look. The whole side of Dave's head was a gory mess.

Lance caught up the horses, loaded the dead marshal on one and mounted the other and set out for Rossiter. Dave had been sent to kill him and the Rossiter bunch had sent him. He knew this, but it was the same old story of no proof.

He came to the outskirts of town and circled until he was directly behind the pretentious residence of Mark Rossiter. He took the body of the marshal in his arms and trudged warily along the side of the house to the front. The street was very dark. He found his way to the big front porch and carefully deposited his burden on the steps. He propped the body against a column and left it there.

The discovery of the body the next morning brought consternation to the members of the

Rossiter Development Company and huge satisfaction to long-suffering citizens. The Company knew for a certainty who was responsible for Dave's death but now discovered how annoying it was to be without proof.

Their consternation, poignant as it was, was nothing to that they experienced that same afternoon. The purchasers of the land were as busy as a colony of ants. Lumber from a sawmill set up by the Company was being hauled and dumped on the sites of homes, men were energetically laying out lines and digging foundations and hauling stone. The creek water rippled merrily along the channels.

Mark Rossiter had been greatly upset by the discovery of the almost faceless Dave and keenly felt the indignity heaped upon him by L. Jefferson Jones when he selected the mayor's residence as a repository for the corpse, but his was a sturdy constitution and recovery was rapid. He swore a fresh oath to exterminate the troublesome Mr. Jones and assembled his fellow officers for a tour of inspection. By this time the settlers would be needing various tools and implements and the bank had money to lend.

They were in the midst of this inspection when they heard a distant *boom* and glanced swiftly in the direction of the *hacienda* to see a huge cloud of smoke and flying dirt and stone. They wondered mildly why the troublesome Mr.

Jones and his tough Texans were blasting and wished that the whole outfit had been destroyed in the explosion. And presently they saw a settler from an adjacent quarter-section running and stumbling towards them, his eyes popping and his arms waving. He came to a halt before them, shaking and heaving.

"The water!" he panted. "It's gone! Somebody changed—course of the creek!"

For a short space utter dismay and confusion reigned; they knew it was true but could not credit it. That the water should fail them had never entered their heads; streams do not change their courses unless some upheaval of nature occurs or men spend laborious hours making new channels. They had done the latter but there had been no indication that L. Jefferson Jones had been preparing to do likewise. The existence of another creek bed had not even been suspected.

The panic-stricken officers of the Company hurried to the nearest ditch; the water level was slowly falling, baring the naked wet soil of the banks. Alarmed settlers began to converge on the place where Rossiter and his partners stood, and one of them demanded, "Mr. Rossiter, what does this mean?"

The full significance of just what this did mean reached him then and for once he lost his aplomb. "I—I don't know," he stammered. A swiftly rising rage choked him then. "It's that Jones fellow! He's changed the course of the creek. But he won't get away with it! I swear to you he won't."

He ran to his waiting buggy and Ordman sprang to the seat beside him; he picked up the reins and struck the startled horse with the whip. The buggy bounced over the uneven ground towards the fence. Bennett, Taylor and Dunn hastened to follow. Wire was hastily stripped away and the vehicles bounced up the valley. The settlers, without transportation, were left behind to discuss this sudden and upsetting turn of events.

It was a long drive and in their state of frantic impatience it seemed longer. When at last the lurching vehicles topped a rise near the ford they could see the water, muddy and dotted with floating brush, winding across the valley towards the gap. They drew up at the edge of the stream; there was no bridge and they were uncertain of the depth of the water. They wrapped reins about whip sockets and leaped to the ground.

A quick glance told them what had happened. A mass of fresh earth and stone blocked the old channel at what had been the ford; more moist earth showed where the explosion had torn out the barrier which had originally turned the creek. The Texans were camped on the far bank; they had fetched along the chuck wagon and were eating supper. They did not even glance towards the furious Rossiter and his stricken partners.

Rossiter stamped angrily along the bank. "Hello, over there! I want to see Jones at once!" They gave him no answer and he yelled again, "I tell you I want to see Mr. Jones!"

Joe Stacy turned his head. "Well, come on over and see him."

Rossiter tightened his lips and stalked back to the buggy. He got in and picked up the reins; the water was only hub deep and they made the crossing easily. Rossiter and Ordman got out and their angry eyes spotted Lance. Rossiter said, "Jones, what right have you to change the course of the creek?"

Lance mopped up his plate and set it aside. He turned his head and said coldly, "This creek comes from a big spring in the hills behind the *hacienda*; it's my water. I decided that I could improve my range by turning it back into its original channel."

"What do you mean, original channel?"

"The creek originally flowed across the valley and through the gap just as it is flowing now. Somewhere along the line a Guiterras thought it would serve him better if it watered the lower end of the valley. The land there was his; now it's passed into other hands and I need the water myself."

"Water is free; you can't deny it to those who need it. It—it's illegal."

Lance gave him a cold smile. "Is it? Ask Ordman."

Rossiter wheeled to the lawyer. "It *is* illegal. Tell him it is."

The lawyer remained silent, his gaze on Lance. Lance said, "Go ahead, Ordman; tell him."

Ordman said, "Look here, Jones; regardless of the legality of the thing consider it from the humanitarian angle. These settlers have invested their money in land which is worthless without water. By withholding that water you're robbing them of their chance to make a living, taking the bread and butter from their mouths."

Lance got up slowly, his face grim. "Did you and your crowd consider the humanitarian angle when you plotted to steal the living from an old man and a girl? Did you consider the humanitarian angle when you set Ben Clark to stealing cattle and thus invite him to kill a man and bring about his own death?"

"We had nothing to do with that!" shrilled Rossiter. "Ben Clark stole those cattle and forged Jacob's name to the bills of sale. We had nothing whatever to do with it."

"You had everything to do with it. Ben confessed to me, told me of your whole scheme. I know he told the truth and so do you."

"You turn that creek back into its channel or

203

I'll sue you for slander! You've made slanderous statements before witnesses and admitted in the same breath that you couldn't prove them!"

"Go right ahead and sue. We'll drag the whole dirty scheme right out into the open for the world to see. You'll have a mighty hard time pinning the guilt on a dead man. Go ahead, Rossiter, and sue."

Ordman put a restraining hand on Rossiter's arm. His gaze was still on Lance. He asked, "What is your price, Jones?"

Lance flashed him a scornful glance. "I have no price. I said I'd pull you from your high places and that's what I'm doing. And I'm going to hang guilt all over you before I get through. I'm not worrying about taking the bread and butter from the mouths of innocent settlers; they won't lose a dime. Rossiter made his public statements, too. One of them was to the effect that if those settlers found the land otherwise than it has been represented the Company would reimburse them. Go right ahead and reimburse."

He turned away and Rossiter started after him with a plea of, "But just a moment, Mr. Jones!" He was no longer arrogant and pompous; he was sweating. But Lance did not turn back and Ordman once more grasped him by an arm and halted him. "No use pleading with him. We're sunk."

The others had been standing in a little group

behind them. Percy Dunn asked anxiously, "But it *is* illegal, isn't it, Jacob!"

Ordman answered shortly. "It's so legal that I wouldn't make myself ridiculous by filing suit against him."

It was a dispirited bunch of conspirators which drove slowly back to town. It was dark when they arrived, but knots of men had gathered in stores and saloons, settlers mingling with citizens, all discussing the master stroke by which this man Jones had crushed the ambitious plans of the Rossiter Development Company.

And now at last the citizens had their day. They told the settlers just what they thought of Rossiter and his gang, they lauded Jones as a man who had done the settlers a favor, reminding the latter that Rossiter had promised to return their money and affirming that had they remained in the valley Rossiter would surely have cleaned them out.

"They'd get you in debt to the bank and give you just enough to live on and never enough to square up and pull out," explained Hank Wetherby. "They're a foxy bunch, but Jones outfoxed 'em. I said he would."

The settlers called in a body on Rossiter and demanded that he make good his promise to them. He greeted them gravely and listened quietly to the demand. On the way back to town he and Ordman had thrashed the thing out;

it looked hopeless but they could make a try. The main thing was to stall for time. Ordman was to leave at once for the hill ranch and try to contact Buck Borden. They would make Borden marshal and swear his gang in as deputies. They might need protection before the thing was done with.

Rossiter had regained some of his assurance. He said to them, "I'm as upset over this unprecedented happening as you are, gentlemen, but things are not as hopeless as they may seem. Jones turned the creek out of spite, personal spite against me for having him run out of town. We'll take legal steps to force him to turn the creek back into its proper channel, and in the meanwhile we're going to start drilling for water. The creek has its origin in a huge spring and there may be an underlying stratum of water which will serve our every purpose. You will be accommodated at the hotel free of charge. I'm sure we will find a solution to our difficulties."

Having talked with the citizens they were somewhat skeptical, but deciding that they had nothing to lose they left and Rossiter breathed a sigh of relief.

The next day a crew started drilling for water and several settlers began digging wells of their own. On the following day Buck Borden rode into town with seven men; he was sworn in as marshal and his men were deputized to assist him in his duties. The crew in the valley kept drilling and the settlers digging. They were down pretty far and had found no sign of the "underlying stratum of water." Discontentment grew.

A day later Rossiter's wife and daughter departed in one of the new Butterfield coaches and Rossiter told his friends they had gone for a few days' shopping in the city. The citizens exchanged sly winks. "Gettin' 'em out of the battle zone," said Hank Wetherby wisely.

Subsequent events seemed to bear out Hank's opinion. Several more days passed and the drilling crew was still getting dust and the settlers had given up digging in despair. There just wasn't any "underlying stratum." They went once more to demand their money and transportation home. The officers of the Development Company had gathered for a conference behind locked doors and Rossiter refused to admit the settlers. Somebody got mad and tossed a rock through a window and the destruction started.

More stones were flung and the windows were shattered. Rossiter snatched up a shotgun and fired through an opening and Ordman cursed him and tore the weapon from his grasp. "You damned fool! Have you lost your senses?"

"I'm trying to summon Borden!" cried Rossiter. "Where is he? What did we hire him for?"

Buck and his gang came on the run and the settlers were dispersed. Somebody threw a stone at Buck and his men opened fire. A settler was wounded in the leg. Armed citizens rushed to the aid of the settlers and Buck ordered his men to cover. The battle was on.

Abner Stacy poked his head out of the door, took a quick look and ran for his horse. He set out at a wild gallop towards the ACC. The crew was still camped at the creek and when he splashed his horse across the stream they were on their feet awaiting him. He did not dismount. He shouted, "Hell's busted loose in Mustang! Them settlers tossed some rocks at Rossiter's house and Buck Borden and his bunch are havin' a reg'lar street battle. By jacks, Lance, it's time you took over."

Lance and his cowboys were already running for their horses.

Abner started the trip back at once, cutting across the range to the Stars and Bars. The Colonel was on the porch and Abner outlined the situation. The Colonel got to his feet, his eyes flashing. "We'll be there, suh!" he promised, and went into the house for his cartridge belt and pistol. As he passed through the kitchen on his way to get his three punchers, Nancy, who was helping Aunt Betsy get supper, asked what had happened. He told her and said sternly, "You stay right here."

She didn't stay right there; when her grandfather and his three retainers galloped from the yard she got her thirty-two and buckled it about her and ran down to the corral. She saddled up and headed for town. She saw the Colonel and his men nearing the road and saw Lance and the Texans rushing to meet them; the two forces joined and swept on towards Rossiter. Nancy followed them.

Darkness was gathering when Lance and the Colonel rode into town at the head of their men. They swept into the street unheralded and, until then, unseen. They couldn't have arrived at a more opportune time, for Buck Borden, determined to end the sniping tactics of the citizens, was leading his men in a charge along the street designed to clear the thoroughfare of settlers and citizens for good and all. Not until the Texans cut loose with a wild rebel yell did Buck see them, and then it was too late to flee.

They met head-on and the fight was furious if short-lived. Buck did not fire a single shot; he cut down on Lance and Colonel Pendleton's big pistol roared and Buck was knocked clear out of his saddle. Several others of his bunch dropped under the Texans' fire before the rest recovered their wits sufficiently to throw away their guns and shove their hands into the air.

In a few minutes the roundup was completed and peace was restored. Lance took command

and at his order the wounded were cared for and the survivors of Buck's outfit were locked in the little jail. With the exception of Rossiter and his friends, who still cowered inside his house, the whole town had assembled in front of the jail, and Hank Wetherby mounted a watering trough and shouted them into silence.

"I figger it's high time we removed the skunks who've been runnin' our town from office. I'm callin' a town meetin' in the hall above the store for the purpose of electin' public-spirited citizens who'll serve without pay. How about it?"

They surged in a body to the hall, a cheering, approving mob. Hank called the meeting to order and in just about five enthusiastic minutes Colonel Pendleton was elected mayor, with Hank, Abner and another citizen named as councilmen. L. Jefferson Jones was unanimously appointed marshal, and when he declined the office was persuaded to take the job until a permanent officer could be found.

And the town was renamed Mustang.

Lance walked up to the Rossiter house and rapped sharply on the door. It was dark now but there was no light in the house. He heard footsteps, then came Rossiter's voice, "Who is it?"

"Jones. The war's over, Rossiter; you can open up."

The door was opened and Lance went in. He walked past Rossiter and entered the front room and struck a match. There was a lamp on a table and he lighted it, then turned to face the men gathered there. He saw Rossiter, Ordman, Bennett, Taylor and Dunn. He said, "Sit down, gentlemen; we've some talking to do."

They found chairs and he stood before them, his gaze moving from one to another of them. He said, "Four years ago I first came to Mustang, a raw, ignorant boy named Lance Jones. I came expecting to find warmth and friendship; if you'll think back you'll remember how I was received."

He paused and watched as remembrance came into their faces; he saw them exchange glances. He went on speaking, telling them the story much as he had told it to Nancy that evening when she came to plead for range.

"The Rossiter Development Company is through but there are wrongs that must be righted. I know and you know that Colonel Pendleton was encouraged to borrow and that his cattle were stolen so that he could not pay back the loans. Some of these cattle have been returned, but this Company is still indebted to him for fifteen hundred head of stock which you had Ben Clark peddle at the ridiculously low price of twenty dollars a head. Pay the Pendletons thirty thousand dollars and I'll call everything square."

"And if we refuse?" sneered Rossiter.

"Then I'll dig and keep digging until I can pin the crime of theft and criminal conspiracy on the whole bunch of you."

"That," said Ordman drily, "I want to see."

"You refuse to make restitution?"

"We refuse to concede that restitution is due. We deny responsibility for the theft of any Stars and Bars cattle. Ben Clark did the rustling and the bills of sale he gave were forged. And you'll never in this world prove otherwise."

He studied them and saw only challenge and defiance on their faces. They had talked it over, had decided to say nothing, to admit nothing. They were sure that he had no proof and that as long as they kept silent he never would have proof.

Lance tried one more angle. "I'm going to make it easy for one of you. The one who comes forward and confesses the plot, revealing it in detail to the proper authorities, will go free. One of you must be wise enough to see that it's the best way out, the only safe way; for sooner or later I intend to prove my charges, and if I have to do it the hard way all of you will suffer the stiffest penalty that the law can impose."

It was sheer bluff and they knew it. Rossiter said, "You can't scare us, Jones. You'll never get a confession when there's nothing to confess. Now you'll oblige us all if you get out of here."

Lance smiled thinly. "I don't want to associate with you any longer than is necessary. I've kept the promise I made at my grandfather's grave, for a town meeting was held tonight and new town officials were elected. You are now very small frogs without any puddle at all. The town has regained its self-respect by taking its old name of Mustang. In case any of you has a change of heart I'll be in the marshal's office until midnight. At that time my offer of immunity to the one who confesses will expire."

He nodded curtly and left the room and they heard the front door close behind him. Ordman said, "He's checkmated; he can't make a move."

"So long as we hang together," added Rossiter. "And hang together we must. We'll sell out here and move to another location suited to our purpose where we can be sure of a satisfactory water supply."

"I'm broke," said Bennett moodily. "What I get for my store and stock will have to go towards setting up in business elsewhere."

"That goes for me too," said Taylor. The others nodded.

Rossiter studied them. He was fairly sure of Ordman, but one of the others might weaken. He said, "I am in a more fortunate position financially than the rest of you and I am inclined to take the blame for our failure. I will make it up to you by advancing any monies needed for another project, permitting you to repay me out of the profits."

That did it. The temptation to confess, to save one's skin at the expense of the others, vanished.

"And the settlers?" asked Ordman grimly.

Rossiter sighed. "We shall have to return their money. If we keep their good will we'll have them as live prospects for the next venture."

They shook hands and separated. They went to their respective homes and ate their belated suppers and were so cheerful about it that their families regained some of their assurance and once more tilted their noses in the air.

Lance was experiencing a deep sense of frustration. He had spoiled their plan to get rich at the expense of the settlers, he had restored some of the loss sustained by the Pendletons; but they were escaping punishment for fraud and theft and would be free to transfer their activities elsewhere. He had torn them from their high places in Mustang but like some malignant weed they would sprout in some other unsuspecting community.

He strode moodily to the jail, saw that his prisoners had been fed and sent the guard to join the rest of the Texans at their camp outside the town. Mustang was tranquil now, with Dave Schultz gone and Buck Borden and his men dead or safe behind bars. On the morrow the settlers would collect what was due them and depart, and with the return of their money would come the belief that Mark Rossiter was a man of his word, a square shooter. If he promoted another project elsewhere they would be first on the sucker list.

He sat in the little office waiting, hoping that one of the bunch would decide to get into the clear by betraying his companions, but even as he waited he knew this would never be. They had nothing to lose by remaining silent.

He waited until nearly one, then got up and went out for a round of the town. The places of business were closed and he tried the doors to be sure their owners had locked up. He tried the front door of the bank in its turn, found it locked and went around to the alley. As a matter of routine he twisted the knob of the rear door and pushed, and to his surprise the door gave before him.

He stood for a moment thinking. There was no light within the building, no sound came from the dark interior. There was just the possibility that whoever had locked up had overlooked the back door. He drew his gun, moved to one side and pushed the door slowly open with an extended foot. Still there was no sound. He stepped through the doorway and moved swiftly to one side where his form would blend with the wall.

He waited there for a full minute, stabbing at the darkness with his eyes, straining his ears;

then, satisfied that the unlocked door was the result of an oversight he turned, shut the door and threw the bolt. He sensed rather than heard the movement on his right and turned swiftly, trying to raise his gun. He was too late; something crashed down on his skull and the firmament exploded. He slumped down without a sound.

He opened his eyes and blinked at the bright light which stabbed at them, and it was a moment or two before he realized that he was staring into the beam of a bull's-eye lantern resting on the floor a few feet from his face. His head pained and his mouth was dry and felt as though it was filled with rags. It was; he had been very thoroughly gagged.

A smooth but grim voice said, "So you're awake, eh? Good. I don't mind admitting that I'm in something of a hurry."

He shifted his gaze and saw a pair of legs near the lantern; he followed them upward with his eyes and found himself looking at Mark Rossiter. Rossiter was holding a big Colt and it was pointed at him. Rossiter said, "I want to make it quite plain, Mr. Jones, that if you do not obey my commands instantly and in silence I will blast you into eternity. There will be no reluctance on my part; I don't like you and if you try to queer *this* plan of mine it will cost you your life."

He bent and picked up the lantern with his left

hand, keeping the Colt trained on Lance. He said, "Get to your knees and then to your feet."

Lance obeyed slowly, watching the man. The beam of light followed his movements and so did the menacing gun. Rossiter moved in back of him and the ray of light shifted and fell on two valises. Rossiter said, "You will pick those valises up and walk into the alley. You will then turn left and keep going until I tell you to stop. And the slightest mistake, Mr. Jones, will mean a bullet in your spine. Go ahead."

Lance walked to the valises and picked them up. His head was spinning and throbbed with each step but he dared not hesitate. Rossiter got behind him, put the lantern on the floor, then gripped him by the slack of his coat. Lance felt the muzzle of the Colt against his spine. He moved forward to the door and Rossiter reached around and opened it. They passed through and Lance heard the click of the lock as Rossiter drew the door shut after him. He turned to the left and started along the alley, the gun at his back.

It was lighter here in the starlight and the silence was heavy. Lance moved carefully, his mind seeking a way of escape and finding none. Rossiter, he knew, would certainly shoot if he made a false move of any kind. He did not even dare stumble. They reached the end of the alley and moved out into open country. Rossiter said,

"Turn right. Those trees at the edge of the creek which you so cleverly altered."

There was a buckboard and a team of horses tied to a tree. Rossiter made him put the valises in the bed of the vehicle, then followed with the gun against his back as he untied the horses. Rossiter said, "You will drive. Get on the seat and put your hands in the air."

Lance obeyed. He was watching and waiting, alert to take any chance which offered. None did. Rossiter got into the buckboard behind him and once more he felt the gun prod him in the back. Rossiter said, "Pick up the reins and drive. Slowly until I tell you to speed up."

Again Lance obeyed. His face was drawn and the pain in his head was forgotten. Rossiter was making the getaway he had probably planned right after the creek was turned and he knew he would have to return the settlers' money. He had even sent his wife and daughter ahead. And Lance suddenly knew just how this trip would end for him. Once far enough away from town Rossiter would pull the trigger which would send a bullet crashing through his spine.

Rossiter said, "Turn and drive over to the road; when you reach it, turn right into it and put them to a trot."

The buckboard bounced over the uneven terrain, lurching and heaving. Rossiter, clinging to the seat rail, kept the gun pressed tightly against Lance's back. The town was a huge shadow to the left, still too close for Rossiter to risk a shot.

The right front wheel dropped into a depression and both Lance and Rossiter were thrown violently to the left. For a brief moment the sixgun lost contact with Lance's back but there was not time enough to act. They reached the road and Lance swung the team to the right and slapped them with the reins. They broke into a trot. Lance began to sweat. If he did anything at all it would have to be soon. In the dim starlight he saw a bend in the road ahead.

They hit it on the run and the horses turned left. Lance and Rossiter swayed to the right and again the pressure of the gun was removed. But this time Lance was waiting for it. Instantly he jerked on the right rein and the horses came out of the left turn to swerve sharply in the opposite direction.

It worked perfectly. Rossiter, entirely unaware, was thrown violently to the left, lost his balance entirely and went sprawling over the rear wheel and into the brush at the side of the road. Lance, prepared, could have retained his seat, but he didn't want to. He let the momentum fling him clear of the vehicle and his hands were extended before him to break his fall. He landed on his stomach and slid a few feet, then rolled once and got up. He wheeled to his left and sprinted. A figure was just erecting itself and Lance hurled himself at it in a flying tackle. A gun roared and the bullet scorched his shoulder; then he hit Rossiter squarely amidships and sent the big man hurtling over backwards.

It was a short struggle. Rossiter felt his gun hand gripped with steel fingers and then came a twist which brought a howl of agony from him. The gun dropped from his hand. Then a fist caught him full on the chin and so much like the kick of a mule was it that the heavy brown beard could not cushion the blow.

Rossiter, in his turn, saw a few stars explode.

Lance drove into Mustang around three in the morning with two valises stuffed with money and securities and valuable papers and Mark Rossiter, somewhat the worse for wear, securely handcuffed to the seat. The first stop was at Abner's house where a hail brought the old fellow out in boots and flannel nightshirt. A terse explanation sent him inside to add trousers and sixgun, after he hurried to the jail. Lance had already locked Rossiter in a cell with some of Buck Borden's boys, and he left Abner to guard them while he rode to the camp after his Texans.

They reentered the town quietly just in time for breakfast at the Taylor House. The Colonel and Nancy were there and after they had finished eating Lance asked them to wait in the lobby.

Nancy eyed him thoughtfully; he was pleased and smiling and she knew that at last he had got some kind of a break. She did not question him.

They were joined in the lobby presently by Jacob Ordman, Caleb Bennett and Percy Dunn, who had been summoned by three of the Texans. They answered the summons out of curiosity, entirely sure of themselves. They did not speak to the Colonel or to Nancy, but kept in a small aloof group. Lance came in with Leander Taylor. He waved them to chairs and said, "Mr. Rossiter is unable to be with us. He is sharing a cell with some of Buck Borden's bunch in our local calaboose."

Ordman came to his feet. "On what charge are you holding him?" he demanded angrily.

"On a charge that I promise you will stick: the charge of embezzlement. Your esteemed president was apprehended this morning while he was trying to sneak out of Mustang with two valises filled with money, securities and some very interesting documents."

That hit them right where they lived. They couldn't believe it at first, but when the valises were opened and Lance had told his story and the Ordman boy came running to say that the bank had been robbed, they saw the light.

It was an abject surrender, each trying to beat the others to it in placing the blame on Rossiter. Rossiter was the brains of the company; it was

Rossiter who had conceived the whole thing; they were the innocent bystanders who had been drawn into the vortex by circumstances beyond their control; it was Rossiter who had suggested the loans and the means of bankrupting the Pendletons; Rossiter who had hired Ben Clark to do the dirty work.

Lance let them spill it all and in the end each was claiming the immunity he had promised to the one who supplied the information.

He said to them contemptuously, "There was a deadline on that confession; it was midnight of last night. You were all in it and can take your chances with the law. You're under arrest. Those Butterfield coaches will come in mighty handy to transport you to Junction City for trial."

The Texans took them down to jail and Lance found himself alone in the lobby with Nancy and the Colonel. He told them, "You'll get back money for the cattle that were stolen, and it won't be at the rate of twenty dollars a head, either. I intend to see to that. And now that the land at the end of the valley is useless to them, I believe you can buy it back for a song. They'll need funds if they hope to put up any kind of a defense against the charges we'll sock against them."

The Colonel said, "Mr. Jones, suh, you are a gentleman. I realized that the very first time I saw you."

Lance looked at Nancy and saw her looking

at him. She opened her lips to speak, but he forestalled her. "I'm proud to hear you say that, Colonel, although there were times when I've acted in a very ungentlemanly manner. But since I've come to know you, sir, I've had a pattern to follow." He smiled and placed a hand affectionately on the Colonel's arm.

"Thank you, suh. And now if you'll excuse me I'll attend to my duties as Mayor of Mustang. I trust that you'll honor us with your company at dinner, Mr.—Confound it, suh, I'd like to call you by your first name."

"It's Lance. Lance Jones."

"An odd name, but a pleasing one, Lance. We'll expect you at dinner."

He moved away gravely and with that inherent dignity which was his and Nancy and Lance looked steadily at each other.

"He didn't remember the name," she said softly.

"I was hoping he wouldn't. He must never know, Nancy."

"My very best friends call me Nance." The color crept into her cheeks but she did not remove her gaze.

"I'd like that. Nance and Lance; they seem to go together."

"Is—is that a suggestion, sir?" She asked it bravely enough and the level gaze did not falter, but the color was deepening.

He reached out and took her hand and held it

223

tenderly between both his own. "Knowing just where I stand, would it be accepted as that?"

She laughed softly then and moved a bit closer to him. The violet eyes were very warm and in them he saw the answer he so much wanted.

He gathered her to him and kissed her.

Center Point Large Print
600 Brooks Road / PO Box 1
Thorndike, ME 04986-0001 USA

(207) 568-3717

US & Canada:
1 800 929-9108
www.centerpointlargeprint.com